Contents

About your adventure

The woods can be frightening when you are on your own. With each step you take, you feel like you're being watched. Has someone come to help you or to do you harm?

In this fairy tale, you control your fate. The seven dwarfs lead the way as you make choices to determine what happens next.

5

Chapter 1 sets the scene. Then you choose which path to read. Follow the directions at the bottom of the page as you read the stories. The decisions you make will change your outcome. After you finish one path, go back and read the others for new perspectives and more adventures.

CHAPTER 1

On the run

All you can hear is your own breath as you run as fast as you can through the forest. There's something behind you. Or so*meone*. You duck behind a tree. All you hear is silence now. Maybe it was just your mind playing tricks on you. Or maybe *she* was playing tricks on you.

You touch the apple in your pocket as your stomach churns with hunger. You wish you had more apples. More food. You don't know how long you'll be out here.

7

Just as you are about to set off into the trees again, a shadow drops across your path. You crouch down as it looms closer. What if it's her? You can't let her find you.

TO BE SECRET AGENT SNOW, WORKING FOR GOOD PRINCE IN A
FUTURISTIC WORLD,
TURN TO PAGE 11.

TO BE A STEPMOTHER SEARCHING FOR YOUR RUNAWAY
STEPDAUGHTER SNOW,
TURN TO PAGE 41.

TO LIVE IN THE ARCTIC WITH YOUR SEVEN LOYAL DOGS,
TURN TO PAGE 75.

CHAPTER 2

Secret Agent Snow and the Seven Robots

"Hunter? Come in, Hunter. White Snow here. Are you there?"

All you hear is crackling on the other end. You hold up your phone to catch a better signal. But the woods are thick and overgrown, and you are far from any mobile phone tower.

You head towards a small clearing you remember passing. Even though you got separated from your partner Hunter, the mission is still the same. Find the Apple.

A war is on between Good Prince and Evil Queen. For many years Good Prince has been ruler of this land. Under his reign homelessness has decreased, every child received a good education and the land was at peace.

That is until Evil Queen rose to power as second-in-command. Evil Queen is greedy and power-hungry. To gain followers she promises them power and riches, but she never actually delivers. She even captures the homeless off the streets and forces them to become her servants, keeping her palace clean and her jewels sparkling.

Now Evil Queen has launched an all-out war to overthrow Good Prince. You are a secret agent in Good Prince's army. Your code name is White Snow.

Just last night Good Prince called you and Hunter to C.A.S.T.L.E., his underground intelligence bunker. He flipped on the large screen in front of you. On the screen was a red-coloured object that looked like a computer monitor, but it wasn't flat. Instead it had a bulbous tube rounding from its back. A large, boat-shaped keyboard jutted from the bottom. You mentally took note of all its characteristics while Good Prince explained.

"This is Apple 2E," he said.

"It looks like an ancient relic!" Hunter exclaimed.

Good Prince went on. "This computer contains a secret code for a bomb. We need to find it before Evil Queen and her cronies do. If they find it first, they could launch the bomb and destroy us all."

The intelligence report indicated that the last signal received from Apple 2E came from Charming Woods, a vast forest covering hundreds of miles. It's where Evil Queen and her cronies hide out. You and Hunter set off immediately. But now you are separated, and he's not answering your calls.

Once you reach the clearing, you catch a signal and open your trusty spy app, Mirror. It contains a sat nav map and can communicate with other agents. Just as you are about to make contact, you hear a crash in the woods behind you. It could be Hunter. Or it could be one of Evil Queen's goons.

You run through the woods and hide behind a tree. You can still hear something behind you. You touch the apple in your pocket. You wish that you had more. You don't know when you'll get a chance to eat a full meal again.

Just as you're about to creep through the trees again, you see a shadow on the ground in front of you. What if it's Evil Queen? You stand still, hoping to blend into the trees. If she sees you, you're doomed.

The shadow moves on, and you let out a sigh of relief. Suddenly you hear the sound of footsteps. They are walking away from you. You could walk towards the sound to see if it's Hunter. Or you could stay hidden.

TO WALK TOWARDS THE FOOTSTEPS,
TURN TO PAGE 16.

TO STAY HIDDEN,
TURN TO PAGE 19.

You silently slip through the trees. Your secret-agent training has taught you how to move without making a sound. As you move towards the sound of the footsteps, you hear Hunter's voice booming through the woods. You rush towards the sound and see him leaning against a tree. He's shouting into his phone.

"No, please! I did exactly as you asked," he cries. "She vanished. I've looked everywhere!"

Suddenly your phone buzzes in your pocket. You wish you had silenced it. Hunter stops talking and glances in your direction. His face reddens, and he quickly puts the phone behind his back.

"White Snow!" he says relieved. "I've been looking for you. I'm glad you're safe. It's dangerous out here."

"Who were you talking to?" you ask.

"Umm . . . a friend. I mean a confidential informant," he says. "We have a lead on Apple."

You wonder why Hunter's being secretive, but he must have a good reason. "We need to stop wasting time and get moving," you say.

You glance at your phone and see a notification from the Mirror app: POSSIBLE SIGNAL SOUTH, the message reads.

"This way," Hunter says, pointing north. "My intel says this will lead us to Apple 2E."

"Mirror says south," you tell him.

But Hunter has started off into the trees. "Come on!" he says.

You start to follow him, then stop. Maybe you'll find Apple 2E faster if you split up.

TO GO WITH HUNTER,
TURN TO PAGE 22.

TO HEAD SOUTH ON YOUR OWN,
TURN TO PAGE 24.

You decide to stay hidden. You can't risk being caught by the enemy. If it's Hunter, you'll find each other eventually.

You listen as the footsteps fade then grow louder again. Whoever it is seems to be walking in circles. As the footsteps grow closer, birds scatter from branches above you. You hear a rabbit scurrying away. Even the animals are spooked. You make yourself as small as possible behind the tree in order to blend in.

Crunch! Crunch! Crunch! The footsteps stop near your hiding spot. You hold your breath. You have no idea if the person can see you. You can only cross your fingers and hope. A long, silent moment passes. Then a strong hand reaches out and grabs your arm.

TURN THE PAGE.

"Ahh!" you cry as you try to spin around. You catch a glimpse of your attacker's face. You know him. Relief floods you. Then he claps a hand over your mouth.

"Hey! What are you doing?" you try to say, but your words are muffled by his hand.

"You and me, we're going on a little trip to see Evil Queen," he says.

You struggle, but he keeps pushing you through the trees. You hear a sound that you recognize. It's his mobile phone. He pulls it from his pocket. You struggle even harder, hoping that you can wriggle free. But his hold is strong.

"What?" he says into the phone. "Yeah, I've got her. You want just the heart? No, that wasn't the deal. If you want it, you can take it." He clicks off the phone and continues pushing you through the woods.

21

"Evil Queen wants your heart. There's no hope for you now," he cackles, as he takes you to Evil Queen's castle.

THE END

TO FOLLOW ANOTHER PATH, TURN TO PAGE 9.

You follow Hunter through the trees. The sky is darkening, and Hunter's path is winding. You no longer know which direction you're going. You feel lost and out of breath trying to keep up.

"Hunter," you gasp, "are you sure this is the right way?"

"The clue is just ahead!" he insists.

As you take another exhausted step behind him, your trouser leg catches on something. You reach down to pull it free, when a metal hand grasps your finger.

A metal hand? you think. You look down, straight into the eyes of a tiny robot.

"What—" you start to say, but the robot holds its finger to its mouth to shush you.

The robot points at a screen on its chest with the message: I WORK FOR GOOD PRINCE. FOLLOW ME. DON'T SAY A WORD.

This might be a trap, you think. You know you are in the midst of Evil Queen's territory. But still you are curious. The robot is so small that you could easily overpower it if things get sketchy.

"You coming?" Hunter calls. You can no longer see him. You can only hear his voice in the distance.

TO FOLLOW THE ROBOT,
TURN TO PAGE 28.

TO CONTINUE FOLLOWING HUNTER,
TURN TO PAGE 31.

"You go your way, and I'll go mine," you call out to Hunter. "Let me know if you find anything."

You head south. The trees grow thicker. You are glad you have Mirror's sat nav signals, otherwise you'd never find your way around.

Suddenly your phone chirps. The battery is low. You reach into your rucksack for the portable charger. With a sinking feeling, you realize Hunter has it. You are out here alone with a dead phone. You continue walking until you see something shimmering in the distance. You head towards it and discover a small, metal door on the side of the hill.

"Hmm," you say. "An abandoned mine shaft?" You push open the door and peer into pitch darkness. You can't see a thing. Apple 2E could be anywhere. You have to check inside.

You wriggle through the door and look around. You are standing in a large, round room with seven small, metal beds. Each one is connected to an outlet.

"Hmm, that's strange," you say to yourself.

You scan the room for Apple 2E. It's not here, but you do see a pile of cords and electronics next to one of the beds. You sort through the pile. Eventually you find a charger and plug in your phone. You sit down on a metal bed to wait. Suddenly you notice a strange smell wafting around you.

What is that? you wonder. You try to stand up, but it's too late. You're already falling into a deep sleep.

Beep! Beep! Beep! The sound jolts you awake. You sit up and see seven small robots surrounding you.

"What are you doing in our docking station?" one of them yells.

Another robot swivels towards you and scans your face. "Identified as Agent White Snow."

"Hello, Agent," the robot says. "We work for Good Prince. I'm Doc Bot, and this is Happy Bot, Bashful Bot, Dopey Bot, Sneezy Bot, Sleepy Bot and Grumpy Bot."

Allies, what luck! you think. You nod hello.

Just then there's a sharp knock on the door. An old woman's voice calls out, "Hello? Anyone home? I have a message for Agent Snow."

You start towards the door, but the robots block your way. "Don't open it," Doc Bot cautions. "It could be a trap."

"Let's go out of the back door and search for Apple 2E instead," Sneezy Bot agrees.

27

The robots may be able to help you find Apple 2E. But what if the message is important?

TO LEAVE WITH THE ROBOTS, TURN TO PAGE 36.

TO OPEN THE DOOR, TURN TO PAGE 38.

Wordlessly, you follow the robot as it whirs through a maze of trees. It leads you to a small door on the side of a hill. The door flies open and out tumbles another tiny robot, then another, and another. Seven robots in all!

"I'm Doc Bot," says the robot that found you. "And this is Sleepy Bot, Happy Bot, Sneezy Bot, Grumpy Bot, Dopey Bot and Bashful Bot. We work for Good Prince."

In all your years working for Good Prince, you've never heard of these robots. You snap a quick photo of them and upload it to the Mirror app.

The app reads: "VERIFIED AS ALLIES OF GOOD PRINCE. PLEASE PROCEED."

Doc Bot tells you that each robot has a special skill to help win the war against Evil Queen. Doc can give medical treatment. Sleepy Bot can make an enemy fall asleep. Sneezy Bot can blow poison goo from its nose. Happy Bot can change a person from evil to good. Dopey Bot can make a person forgetful. Bashful Bot can make someone hide in fear, and Grumpy Bot is a bomb that explodes when its face turns red.

"We need to work together to find Apple 2E," Doc Bot tells you. "And we know just where to begin."

"But what about my partner Hunter?" you ask.

The robots are silent for a moment. Then Happy Bot pipes up. "We don't think he can be trusted," it says.

As if on cue, your phone buzzes. It's a call from Hunter. "Come quickly!" he says. "I found something!"

"On my way," you say, and click the phone off. The robots are staring at you.

"Could it be a trap?" Doc Bot wonders.

You think for a moment. Hunter *was* acting strangely, leading you on a winding trail through the woods.

"Finding Apple 2E is of the highest importance," Sneezy Bot says.

You agree and think that Hunter could have a lead, even if he *might be* working for Evil Queen.

TO LEAVE AND FIND HUNTER,
GO TO PAGE 31.

TO GO WITH THE ROBOTS,
TURN TO PAGE 33.

You stomp through the woods to find Hunter. He's standing on the edge of a cliff.

"Hunter!" you call to him. "What is going on?"

He waves at you to come closer. When you reach his side, he points at something far ahead. Across the valley you see a tall, black palace on the top of a hill. You recognize it immediately.

"Evil Queen's palace!" you exclaim, turning to Hunter. "But what–"

Suddenly your voice has a sharp echo. You take a step towards Hunter but run into something solid. A glass wall. You turn in the other direction, but hit another glass wall. You realize with dread that you are trapped inside!

31

TURN THE PAGE.

You pound on the glass. "Hunter! What have you done?" you cry. Hunter only looks at you and smirks. You can't believe Hunter, your trusted partner, turned on you and Good Prince. "Traitor!" you shout.

"Take White Snow away!" Hunter calls into the air. Suddenly dozens of armed Evil Queen soldiers run out from the trees and lift the case. They tilt it sideways and you fall over, smacking your head hard against the glass. You see stars.

It's like a glass coffin, you think just as everything goes black. You are carried away as a prisoner of war.

THE END

TO FOLLOW ANOTHER PATH, TURN TO PAGE 9.

You and the robots prowl through the woods looking for any sign of Apple 2E. As night comes you are about to give up until morning. Suddenly your Mirror app beeps. It reads: SIGNAL DETECTED. You and the robots scurry towards the location.

As you approach you see a figure in the trees. It's Evil Queen! The Apple 2E's screen glows with a greenish light in front of her.

"Curses!" Evil Queen mutters, punching the computer keys. "I can't crack the code!"

You see your chance. "Robots, attack!" you shout.

The robots lunge at Evil Queen, beeping angrily. Evil Queen is taken by surprise, but she doesn't look afraid. "You silly robots can't defeat me!" she screams.

"That's what you think, Evil Queen," you yell. "Dopey, let her have it!"

Dopey Bot takes aim and shoots a laser straight at the queen's forehead. Direct hit! The force knocks Evil Queen to the ground. She groans and struggles to sit up.

"Where am I? *Who* am I?" Evil Queen asks with one hand on her forehead. The other is still holding on to Apple 2E. "And what am I holding?"

"Oh you're holding that for me," you say quickly. "But I'll take it back now." You grab the Apple 2E and hoist it up onto your shoulders. "Good Prince thanks you for your assistance."

"Um . . . sure. I mean of course! Anything to help a prince," Evil Queen says, still confused.

You tell the robots to watch Evil Queen, and you head towards C.A.S.T.L.E. and Good Prince. Once there you are treated as a hero.

"Excellent work, Snow," Good Prince says. "You saved the day."

After you leave C.A.S.T.L.E., you pull out your phone. "Mirror, Mirror in my hand," you say. "Who is the greatest secret agent in the land?"

You read Mirror's answer loud and clear: SNOW, WHITE SNOW.

THE END
TO FOLLOW ANOTHER PATH, TURN TO PAGE 9.

You and the robots hike into the woods. But as night falls, you get separated. You climb a small path to the top of a hill. As you near the top, you see an old woman crouched along the path holding an apple.

"Ah, Agent. I've been expecting you," she says as you come near. "I work for Good Prince. I have the item that you seek."

The woman steps away and reveals the Apple 2E behind her. You've found it! Good Prince will be so pleased.

"My, you must be famished," the woman says. "Here, I have an apple. Eat before you start your journey back to C.A.S.T.L.E."

You are a bit hungry, but you need to get moving. "I'm sorry, I have to get back to Good Prince."

"How about half the apple then?" the old woman asks. She slices the apple with a small knife and gives one half to you. She bites into her half, licking her lips. "Delicious!" she says.

Watching the old woman eat makes you hungry. You take a bite of your apple half and swallow. Suddenly the old woman springs to her feet, cackling. She rips off her grey wig, revealing glossy, blonde hair. It's Evil Queen in disguise!

"That's the last apple you'll ever eat!" she cries. A sharp pain pierces your gut.

"You poisoned me!" you exclaim, as you fall to the ground. You can no longer feel your arms and legs. You fall into a deep, poisoned sleep as Evil Queen takes Apple 2E away.

37

THE END

TO FOLLOW ANOTHER PATH, TURN TO PAGE 9.

Maybe the woman's message is important. Your phone has been dead this whole time. What if Good Prince has been trying to contact you?

You step around the robots and fling open the door. A woman with a scarf around her face hobbles in. Just as you are about to ask for the message, Sleepy Bot shoots the woman with its sleep tranquilizers. She slumps to the floor.

"What did you do?" you cry angrily. You run to the woman's side and pull her scarf from her face. It's not an old woman at all. It's Evil Queen!

"I told you it was a trap!" Grumpy Bot barks.

"That was close! Great work, robots," you say, as the robots tie up the sleeping queen.

Even though Evil Queen is no longer a threat, your work is not over. You still need to find Apple 2E and deliver it to Good Prince. You wonder if Hunter has had any luck.

"Thanks for your help!" You wave at the robots as you step out of the door to the woods.

You reach for your phone, now fully charged, and call Hunter so you can search together. Now that Evil Queen has been captured, there's no rush. You might even enjoy looking for Apple 2E now. You set off on your search, whistling while you work.

THE END

TO FOLLOW ANOTHER PATH, TURN TO PAGE 9.

Runaway Snow

You've just got home from a long day of work. Your stepdaughter Snow is nowhere in sight. She must be listening to rock music in her bedroom again. You decide not to bother her. You and Snow used to be very close. She even chose to live with you after you and her father split up. But lately Snow has been grouchy and sullen.

You decide to make an apple tart for her as a treat. Snow loves apples. You are just getting out the ingredients when the doorbell rings. At the door is Wally Mirror, a boy from Snow's class. He holds up his rucksack.

41

"I'm here to work on a group project with Snow," Wally tells you. You hope Wally will cheer Snow up. She has a huge crush on him, but Wally is completely clueless. You rush to Snow's bedroom to tell her. You knock on her door, but she doesn't answer. She must be wearing her headphones.

"Wally's here," you say opening the door.

"What?" she yells.

"Can you take those off?" you shout pointing to her ears.

42   "But this is my favourite Septuplets song!" she protests, pulling her headphones down.

"Wally's here," you repeat.

Snow turns to peer into the mirror over her dresser. She stares at her reflection and frowns. She doesn't think she's very pretty.

"My hair is too dark," Snow pouts. "My skin is too pale. My lips are too red."

"You're beautiful," you say.

Snow sighs then grabs her laptop and heads downstairs, where Wally is waiting. Wally and Snow sit at the kitchen table to work on the project while you continue making the tart.

Wally turns to Snow and whispers, "Wow, your stepmum is *so* pretty. I bet she's the prettiest person in town!"

Snow snaps her laptop shut. "Let's finish tomorrow," she says irritably.

43

Wally looks surprised. "Um, OK. See you–"

"Yeah, bye," Snow interrupts, then runs up to her room and slams the door.

After Wally leaves, you knock on Snow's door. She flings it open, tears streaming down her face.

"It's all your fault!" Snow yells. "You're the pretty one. Not me! I can't live here anymore." She grabs her duffel bag and pushes past you down the hall and out of the front door.

"Wait!" you cry, running after her, but Snow doesn't slow down.

By the time you reach the pavement, you don't see Snow anywhere. You think she might have gone to the nearby woods to hide. It was always her favourite place as a little girl. You run as fast as you can into the woods. You touch the apple in your pocket as your stomach churns with hunger. You never did get a chance to eat that apple tart.

Just as you are about to set off into the trees again, a shadow drops across your path. It grows bigger and bigger. Two faces peer around a tree trunk at you. It's your neighbour's boys, Will and Jacob Grimm.

"Hey, Ms White!" they exclaim. "What are you doing out here?"

45

"Looking for Snow," you tell them. "Have you seen her?"

The Grimm brothers look at each other. "She said she was running away and never coming back," Jacob finally mumbles.

"Do you know where she's going?" you ask.

"Didn't say," Will answers.

You know you need to find Snow before she gets too far. She could be at Fairy Park, her favourite park in the city. But if she *really* wants to run away, she might be at the train station. It's the fastest way out of town.

46

TO SEARCH IN FAIRY PARK,
GO TO PAGE 47.

TO GO TO THE TRAIN STATION,
TURN TO PAGE 50.

You decide to head to town and search Fairy Park. The park stretches over several city streets. You'd forgotten how huge the park is. Snow could be anywhere.

You enter the gates. The park is jam-packed with people carrying drinks, eating food and having a good time. On a stage at the far end of the park, a rock band is playing. You tap someone on the shoulder.

"What's going on?" you ask.

"Fairy Fest," he yells over the music. "The park's biggest music fair."

"Oh, no," you groan. It's going to be much more difficult to find Snow among all these people. But you are also relieved. Snow loves music, so she's bound to be here somewhere. But where?

As you move through the crowd, the band on stage begins a new song. The band looks familiar, but you can't quite place them. Then you realize you've seen their poster hanging on Snow's bedroom wall. It's the Septuplets, her favourite band!

The Septuplets could help me find Snow, you think.

You elbow through the crowd to get closer to the stage. You still have a long way to go when the song ends. Oh, no! The band is starting to pack up their equipment. You try to move faster, but the huge crowd is tough to push through. At this rate you may never catch the band.

As you move through the crowd, vendors call out to you trying to sell their goods – fresh fruit, beautiful hair combs and band T-shirts.

You are struck with an idea. Snow has never been able to resist food and shiny trinkets. You could pose as a vendor and bring her right to you. Or you could keep trying to catch the Septuplets.

TO POSE AS A VENDOR SELLING ITEMS,
TURN TO PAGE 52.

TO KEEP GOING TOWARDS THE SEPTUPLETS,
TURN TO PAGE 54.

You know that if Snow is determined to run away, she'll try to get as far away as possible. The train station is the best place to look. You have to catch her before she has a chance to board a train.

When you reach the station, you are amazed at how big it is. You stare at the huge monitors that list all the departures. Which train would she take?

You approach the ticket counter and pull out a picture of Snow. "Have you seen this girl?" you ask the two ticket attendants.

The male attendant peers at the photograph and shrugs. "I don't remember."

The female attendant points at something behind you. "Maybe you should ask him," she suggests.

You whirl around. On the wall behind you is a poster of a man in a suit holding a magnifying glass. It reads:

On the hunt for someone?

Call Theo Huntsman, Private Investigator.

You could use help finding Snow. But you still might be able to find her on your own.

51

TO CALL THEO HUNTSMAN,
TURN TO PAGE 64.

TO SEARCH THE TRAIN STATION ON YOUR OWN,
TURN TO PAGE 67.

You decide to try luring Snow to you by selling the things she loves. You walk towards the vendor stands lined up on the edge of the park.

"Apples and fruits galore!" one seller calls out.

"Get your beautiful jewelled combs here!" another shouts.

You approach the fruit stand and comb sellers. "Would either of you like a break?" you ask. "I could take over for a while. I'm a good salesperson!"

"I would love a break!" the fruit seller exclaims.

"So would I!" says the comb seller. "I've been here all day."

You look from one to the other. Your stepdaughter absolutely loves apples, and she's probably hungry. But she'd also want a shiny, jewelled comb for her hair.

53

TO SELL FRUIT,
TURN TO PAGE 59.

TO SELL JEWELLED COMBS,
TURN TO PAGE 61.

You decide to try to catch the Septuplets before they leave the park. You weave through the crowd of people towards the stage, ignoring the cries of vendors and stepping on people's toes. Finally, breathless, you reach the stage just as the band members have loaded the last of their stuff into an old wood-panelled van.

"Wait!" you cry.

The Septuplets stop and turn towards you. One band member stretches her arms out and yawns. Another sneezes.

A third smiles at you. "Hello!" she says.

Another girl sighs and rolls her eyes. "Oh great, another fan who wants an autograph. Let's just go."

"No, no, I'm not a fan," you say.

The seven girls stare at you. Your cheeks flush with embarrassment. "I mean . . . that's not why I'm here. I need your help." You tell the Septuplets about Snow, Wally and the whole misunderstanding.

"Oh, that's awful!" one Septuplet says. "We'd love to help."

You sigh, relieved. The girls introduce themselves as Coy, Bliss, Simple, Dozy, Snappy, Medic and Sniffle.

The girls start brainstorming ideas. "We could write a song telling Snow to come home," Simple offers.

"That would take too long," Snappy argues.

"I say search the wooded area of Fairy Park. She's probably hiding," Coy says from behind her long fringe.

"Throw a party!" Bliss suggests cheerily. "She'll definitely come home for a party."

Your mind is reeling. All the girls have great suggestions, but you don't know which one would be the best.

56

TO TAKE BLISS' ADVICE, AND THROW A PARTY,
GO TO PAGE 57.

TO TAKE COY'S ADVICE, AND SEARCH THE WOODS,
TURN TO PAGE 70.

You decide to throw a party, and you invite the Septuplets to play in your back garden. You know Snow would never be able to resist a party, especially if her favourite band is playing. You'll even make her favourite apple tarts. The Septuplets help you hang flyers around town. You call Ethan Printz, Snow's good friend, and tell him to post details of the party online.

The day of the party, you bake seven apple tarts. The smell of the sweet puddings wafts through the air. The Septuplets rock out in your back garden, and the house fills with people. Ethan Printz is there, along with Snow's other friends. Even the Grimm brothers show up to write about the party on their blog.

57

TURN THE PAGE.

Finally the door opens, and Snow walks in. "Whoa! Is that really the Septuplets playing in our garden?" she asks.

You wrap her in a big hug. "I threw this party just for you!" you tell her.

"Thanks!" she says. Then she frowns. "Is Wally Mirror here?" she asks.

"Forget him," you say. "You don't need a boy to tell you that you're beautiful and loved."

Snow gobbles up a piece of tart and goes out to the garden to dance. You watch her, smiling. Maybe now you can all live happily ever after.

58

THE END

TO FOLLOW ANOTHER PATH, TURN TO PAGE 9.

You tell the fruit seller to take a break and take her place behind the fruit stand. You pull a hat low over your face and conceal yourself with bushels of apples. You scan the crowd. You don't see a single person who looks like Snow.

"Apples! Fresh-picked apples!" you call shrilly, disguising your voice as much as you can. "Red ones, green ones. Tart and juicy!"

You hope that somewhere in the crowd, Snow will hear you and come running. All the shouting is making your throat hurt.

Suddenly you spot Snow wandering past. "Miss! Miss!" you cry in a squeaky voice. "A free apple for you, the fairest of them all!"

Snow stops and turns to you. You dangle the apple in front of you. Snow moves towards you and reaches for the apple.

You drop the apple into Snow's hand, revealing your face. "Snow, please come home," you say.

Snow rolls her eyes. "Oh, it's you," she says eating the apple. "Fine, I'll come home. But only if I can bring my friends." She gestures behind her, and the entire Septuplets band comes forward. "They need a practice space," Snow tells you excitedly. "I told them our garage would be perfect!"

You are happy to have Snow home again, but you are not so happy about the Septuplets practising in your garage. Your whole house rocks long into the night. But that's not even the worst part. A lot of their songs seem to involve whistling, which is really getting on your nerves.

THE END

TO FOLLOW ANOTHER PATH, TURN TO PAGE 9.

Snow loves wearing shiny combs and barrettes in her hair. She'll no doubt be drawn to the jewelled comb booth.

"I'll take your place for a while," you tell the comb seller. You hop into the stand and decorate your hair with beautiful combs. Then you wrap a scarf around your face and scan the crowd.

"Jewelled combs for sale!" you call, disguising your voice. Finally you see Snow moving through the crowd. "Hello there, Miss!" you cry. "Would you like to try on some jewellery?"

As Snow turns, you see that she is already wearing several jewelled combs in her hair. Still, she marches towards the stand. You are overjoyed until you see the angry look on her face.

"You can't fool me," she snaps. "I know it's you."

You slowly unwrap the scarf from your face and sigh. "Come home, Snow," you plead.

Snow shakes her head. "Not a chance!" she says. "I'm going to stay with Dad for a while."

Snow twirls away towards the fruit stand and buys a sketchy-looking apple. You sigh miserably. You hope she doesn't end up with food poisoning.

THE END

TO FOLLOW ANOTHER PATH, TURN TO PAGE 9.

You know you need all the help you can get. You dial Theo Huntsman's number and wait for him to pick up.

"Huntsman, at your service," he says.

You explain the situation, and he tells you to come to his office. When you arrive he writes down your information and places it on top of one of the many piles on his desk. You wonder how he can keep track of anything.

"I'll call you with any leads," he says.

The next morning Theo Huntsman calls

you to come to his office. "I've found something!" he says.

When you get to his office, you see that he's holding a small box. You reach for it, but he shoves it behind his back. "Fifty pounds," he says.

You hand him the money, and he opens the box. He holds up a necklace with a heart-shaped pendant.

"What is this?" you ask.

"That's Snow's heart," he tells you, "from the woods."

You shake your head. "No. This isn't Snow's," you say.

Theo Huntsman frowns. "What are you talking about? Of course this belongs to Snow."

You shake your head again. "I think I'd know Snow's heart when I see it."

"Oh," Theo says. "Well if you want me to keep searching, I'll need more money for expenses."

You're not sure Theo Huntsman is worth the money you've paid him. But he may be your only hope. The only other option is to conduct your own search. The woods by Fairy Park would be a good place to start. It's Snow's favourite park.

TO SEARCH FAIRY PARK YOURSELF,
TURN TO PAGE 70.

TO PAY THEO HUNTSMAN TO KEEP SEARCHING,
TURN TO PAGE 72.

You don't have time to waste if you want to find Snow. You start running towards the departure train platforms.

"Ma'am!" the male attendant calls after you. "You need a ticket first!"

You ignore him and leap over the barriers. You hear the attendant's footsteps behind you, but you soon lose him in the crowd of passengers waiting for their trains. You wave a picture of Snow in people's faces.

"Have you seen this girl?" you ask. A tall man looks at the photo and points to a train about to depart. As you are about to run, you stop.

How am I going to get Snow off the train? you wonder. Just then you see one of Snow's friends, Ethan Printz. You've got an idea.

"Ethan, over here!" you say waving the boy down. Ethan strides towards you, looking confident and regal.

"Hi, Ms White. What's wrong?" Ethan asks. You tell him that Snow is running away on the train. You point towards it as the whistle blows.

"Hurry! It's departing!" you cry.

Ethan walks briskly towards the train. You follow, trying to stay out of sight. You can see Snow through the train's glass window. She's slumped in her seat, fast asleep. The train slowly pulls out of the station. Ethan holds up his hand, and the train squeals to a stop. The conductor leaps off the train. That's right! You forgot the Printz family owns most of the train lines.

From behind a pillar, you watch as Ethan steps aboard. You see him reach Snow and gently wake her up. As the pair leave the train, you swear you see a spark between them.

I suppose it doesn't matter what Wally Mirror thinks after all, you think.

THE END
TO FOLLOW ANOTHER PATH, TURN TO PAGE 9.

You decide to search the woods in Fairy Park. Snow has always loved the woods. You take a deep breath and enter. You hope there aren't any wild animals here. Your eyes dart about, watching for any sign of Snow.

"Snow! Where are you?" you shout.

Then you hear someone singing. You move towards the sound. As you peer through the trees, you see Snow on a tree swing. The Grimm brothers are taking turns pushing her. She's singing to the squirrels that leap from branch to branch. You step out from behind the trees.

"Snow!" you cry. Snow jumps off the swing and starts to run away. "Wait! Please come home!" you beg.

Snow pauses, considering. You dig in your pocket and find your apple. You hand it to her.

Snow smiles. "An apple! My favourite! I am pretty hungry." She snatches the apple and devours it happily.

As she eats, you approach the Grimm brothers. "Did you know where she was this whole time?" you demand.

The brothers shrug guiltily. "We just wanted to help her," one says.

"We were going to write about her adventures in our blog," the other adds.

You shake your head at them. "Come on, Snow," you say. "Let's go home."

THE END

TO FOLLOW ANOTHER PATH, TURN TO PAGE 9.

You would pay anything to have Snow back. You hand over more money to Theo Huntsman. "I'll do what I can," he promises.

Several days pass. Then you receive a letter from Theo Huntsman. "I found her!" is written on the envelope.

You tear open the letter. Inside is a postcard of a castle nestled on a mountaintop. You flip the postcard over and see Snow's handwriting. The card is addressed to you. You sigh, thinking of all the money you gave Theo Huntsman for a postcard that would have come to you anyway. It reads: *Dear Mum,*

Guess what? I'm living in a castle! It's really a school for girls. Dad enrolled me. I feel like a princess! Maybe you can visit someday.

Love, Snow.

Someday seems so far away. You hang the
postcard on the fridge and sigh again. At least
Snow is living happily ever after.

THE END

TO FOLLOW ANOTHER PATH, TURN TO PAGE 9.

CHAPTER 4

Meteorologist Snow-White and the Evil Queen of Blizzards

"Help! Please help!" a voice cries on your mobile phone. It's your friend and mentor, Meteorologist Snow-White.

"What's wrong, Snow-White?" you say into your phone.

"It's the blizzard to end all blizzards. The Evil Queen of Blizzards! The weather station is getting buried under all this snow. I'm trapped!" Snow-White cries.

"On my way!" you say. Snow-White has been teaching you everything she knows about weather. One day you hope to be a meteorologist just like her. Plus she's your best friend. You have to help her.

You peek out of the window. All you can see is a sea of white. But that's not unusual since you and your family, the Charmings, live in the Arctic. You live far from civilization. The only way to get anywhere is by dogsled.

Your seven sled dogs are stretched out on their seven beds in front of the fireplace. You've raised the dogs since you found them as puppies, abandoned in an old cottage. They all look alike, but you can tell them apart. You named them based on their personalities: Doc, Grumpy, Bashful, Sleepy, Sneezy, Dopey and Happy. Doc is the lead dog and always takes care of the others.

You bundle up and whistle for the dogs to wake up. The dogs leap to attention, except for Sleepy. She just rolls over and buries her face in her paws. You give her a gentle nudge.

77

When the dogs are ready, you open the door and step out into the bitter wind. The Evil Queen of Blizzards hasn't reached your house yet, but you can see the storm coming your way. You know Snow-White's weather station is in the thick of the storm. You need to get to her quickly. She's all alone out there.

You and the dogs traipse through the woods near your house. The trees are too thick to ride the sled, so you pull it behind you. The sky darkens. All you can hear is your own breathing and the dogs panting as you quicken your pace through the trees. You think you hear something behind you. You imagine the Evil Queen of Blizzards looming over you, ready to touch down and bury you in a mountain of snow. You duck behind a tree to catch your breath.

All you hear is silence now. Maybe your mind was playing tricks on you. You touch the apple in your pocket as your stomach churns with hunger. You wish you had more apples. More food. You don't know how long you'll be out here.

You start off again into the trees, the dogs at your heels. When you reach the trail to the weather station, you tie the dogs' leads to the front of the sled. Before you hop on, you pull out your binoculars.

Uh oh, you think. The storm is right in your path. You could take another trail around it, but you'd risk not getting to Snow-White in time.

TO GO AROUND THE STORM,
TURN TO PAGE 80.

TO TAKE THE DIRECT PATH TO SNOW-WHITE,
TURN TO PAGE 82.

You decide it's too dangerous to venture straight into the path of the storm. Your storm-watching skills tell you that you could head east, where the storm is weakest. Then you could double-back to the weather station.

You shake the dogs' reins and they run across the small rolling hills. Even though the storm is weaker to the east, the wind is still harsh and stirs up snow. It is nearly blinding. The dogs strain to pull you through the terrible wind. As you round a hill, you spot dark, moving shapes in the distance.

80   "Whoa," you say to the dogs. They slow to a stop, and you take out your binoculars again. A group of men is coming over the hills on horseback. The leader is carrying a flag with a large "H" on it.

At the sight of the flag, your heart freezes in your chest. It's the Huntsmen, a notorious gang of roving thieves. They are legendary and vicious – robbing homes and travellers. They'll take anything they can get their hands on. You know that if they find you, they'll take your dogs and your sled. They'll probably even take the half-eaten apple in your pocket.

You peer through the binoculars again. The Huntsmen are headed straight towards you. You remember seeing a cave a bit further back where you and the dogs could hide. Or you could try to outrun them.

81

TO HIDE IN THE CAVE,
TURN TO PAGE 84.

TO MAKE A RUN FOR IT,
TURN TO PAGE 99.

You need to get to Snow-White as quickly as possible. The most direct path is through the storm. You snap the dogs' reins and plunge forward.

The wind howls and the snow swirls as you push on through the storm. The snow is so thick, you can barely see the dogs a few feet in front of you. The icy snow stings your eyes and face. You stop to rub your eyes with your glove. Suddenly you see something moving in front of you. You look sideways and see an apple rolling away across the ice.

An apple? you think. You peer into the distance and see what looks like huge crates of apples. Why would all those apples be out here in the Arctic? Are you dreaming?

Then you hear a voice up ahead. "Where are you?" someone shouts. "I can't see anything!"

"Over here!" says another voice.

This time you know it's not your imagination. These people could be lost out here in the storm. Maybe you could help them. Then again, Snow-White is still in danger. You think of the crates of apples. You could use the food and so could Snow-White.

83

TO HEAD TOWARDS THE VOICES,
TURN TO PAGE 87.

TO CHECK OUT THE APPLES,
TURN TO PAGE 90.

You decide to head towards the cave. It's hidden from view, and the Huntsmen aren't likely to find you there.

You and the dogs duck inside. It is pitch black, and you can't see a thing. Your dogs huddle around you for warmth. Then Grumpy starts growling and straining at his lead. Bashful hides his face in his paws and whines.

You click on your torch to see what the fuss is about. The cave is lined with treasures – gold, jewellery, furs and stacks of money. With dread you realize you are in the Huntsmen's hideout. It's too late to run. You hear the Huntsmen at the cave's entrance. You pull the dogs to the corner of the cave, out of sight, and tell them to stay. There's no way you're letting the Huntsmen take them.

The leader steps inside and shines his torch on your face. "What have we here?" he says to his cronies, who have piled into the cave behind him. "A thief!"

"I'm no thief!" you protest, but the Huntsmen ignore you. They grab your arms and tie you up.

The ropes are tight around your chest. You can barely breathe. You know you are doomed. The Huntsmen cackle with laughter as they exit the cave, leaving you to die.

Late that night you wake to something pulling at your ropes. Wet noses nuzzle your arms and sloppy tongues lick your hands. The dogs! They gnaw at the rope knots until finally you are free. You and the dogs slip quietly out of the mouth of the cave.

When you get outside, the night is clear. You still have to get to Snow-White, but the storm and the Huntsmen are gone.

THE END

TO FOLLOW ANOTHER PATH, TURN TO PAGE 9.

86

You motion for the dogs to follow and move through the thick snowflakes towards the voices. Happy jumps eagerly through the snow. Doc hangs back and scratches at your leg. He's trying to tell you something, but you're not sure what. You just keep blindly moving forward.

"Hello!" you call into the wind. "Over here!" You're not sure if they heard you. The voices are still talking. You can just make out what one of them is saying.

"I can't believe you lost our entire haul!" one man yells. "I risked my neck to rob that place!"

You freeze. You realize you've stumbled across the Huntsmen, a notorious gang of robbers. The Huntsmen scour the Arctic, stealing anything they can get their hands on. No one has been able to catch them.

"Wait. Did you hear something?" another voice says.

Uh oh, you think.

"Hello!" the Huntsmen call into the wind.

Just then Sneezy lets out a giant *Achoo!* "Hush!" you tell him, but it's too late. Through the white shield of snow, you can see several dark figures moving towards you.

You have two choices – run or try to talk to them. You're not sure how fast you can go in this snow. You might be able to use the Huntsmen to find Snow-White. But they are dangerous, and there's no telling what they'll do.

TO TALK TO THE HUNTSMEN,
TURN TO PAGE 95.

TO RUN,
TURN TO PAGE 99.

88

You tug on the dogs' reins to turn them towards the apples. As you get closer, the crates grow more solid in shape. You reach for a red apple and try to take a bite. It's ice cold and rock hard.

"Ouch," you say. You stuff your pockets with apples. Hopefully they will warm up on your way to Snow-White. Suddenly you hear voices again. This time they are closer.

"The stash is around here somewhere," one voice says.

"Find it!" the other growls. "We stole too much to lose it now."

Stolen apples? you think. Of course! This is the work of the Huntsmen, a band of thieves who roam the Arctic robbing every home and village they find.

The police have been looking for the Huntsmen for years, but they always manage to stay under the radar.

You duck behind the crates and listen. From the sound of it, there are only two of them. You might be able to take them on. You gather as many apples as you can. One slips from your arms and rolls through the snow. Dopey bounds after it, thinking it's a ball.

"Come back!" you hiss.

As it turns out, Dopey has done you a favour. The Huntsmen come into view, but they are distracted by Dopey. They don't notice you behind the crates. You stand, take aim and pelt the men with the frozen apples.

91

TURN THE PAGE.

92

Bam! Bam! The surprised men fall over, clutching their heads. You leap from behind the apple crates and tie their hands together with your dogs' reins. You fasten the reins to the back of the sled and drag the Huntsmen behind you.

"Our leader will have your head for this!" one of them cries.

When you reach the top of the hill, you check your mobile phone for a signal. It works! You dial the police and tell them you've captured two of the Huntsmen.

After some time you hear the sound of a helicopter. You wave it down, and it lands nearby. A police officer jumps out and slaps handcuffs on the two men.

"Off to jail for you," the officer says to the Huntsmen.

"We need to make another stop," you say, as you climb into the helicopter. "Meteorologist

Snow-White is trapped in the weather station."

"You heard him," the officer says to the pilot. "Someone's trapped in the snow."

You give yourself a little pat on the back. You certainly feel like the hero in this story.

THE END

TO FOLLOW ANOTHER PATH, TURN TO PAGE 9.

You decide to talk to the Huntsmen. But what will you say? Suddenly you get an idea.

"Hello!" you call.

The Huntsmen charge towards you. The leader is on a huge black horse. "Where are you going, kid?" the leader asks.

"I'm looking for treasure," you say. "Can you help me get there?"

The Huntsmen leader raises his eyebrows. "Treasure, huh?"

You nod eagerly. "Yes! I've seen it – gold, silver and jewels! There's too much for me to carry on my own. If you help me, you can keep part of the treasure."

The leader thinks for a moment. Greed fills his eyes. "OK, kid," he says. "Show us the way."

The leader pulls you up onto his horse, and you call for the dogs to follow behind. You give the gang directions, and the posse sets off across the snowy trail. Soon you near your destination. On a small hill sits a huge mound of snow. Buried underneath is the weather station, but only you know that. You point towards the snow pile.

"There's the buried treasure!" you tell the leader. You cross your fingers and hope that Snow-White will catch on to your plan.

The Huntsmen gallop towards the station. The leader orders you to stay on the horse. He and the rest of the Huntsmen begin to dig in the snow.

"I've found something!" one Huntsman cries. "It's a glass door."

"Well, open it!" the leader orders.

The Huntsmen pull open the door and rush inside. You leap off the horse just as Snow-White runs out of the door. She slams the door behind her and turns the key. The leader's face is pressed up against the glass as he pounds on the door. He and the rest of the Huntsmen are trapped. You give him a little wave.

"They won't be getting out of there for a while," Snow-White chuckles. "Thanks for coming to my rescue, Charming!"

"Nothing to it!" you say with a grin.

THE END

TO FOLLOW ANOTHER PATH, TURN TO PAGE 9.

You whirl around and take off in the opposite direction of the Huntsmen. Doc leads the way, and Grumpy jumps onto the sled. He is protecting you. You can hear the Huntsmen chasing you, but then they stop. Phew! They must have lost you in the snow. You're safe. But now *you* are lost in a world of white. You can't see a thing.

You keep plunging through the billowing snow. The Evil Queen of Blizzards is pummelling you. You know you and the dogs should take cover, but you're nearly to the weather station. It's only an hour's trek, maybe less. Still, the Evil Queen could kill you in minutes, and it's starting to get dark.

TURN THE PAGE.

Suddenly you see a faint flicker of light. Could there be a house out here in the wilderness, or is it just a reflection in the snow? You could check it out, but it's in the opposite direction of the weather station.

TO CHECK OUT THE LIGHT,
GO TO PAGE 101.

TO KEEP GOING TO THE WEATHER STATION,
TURN TO PAGE 104.

You stumble towards the flickering light. If it's a cabin, the owners might help you to rescue Snow-White. It's worth a try. Sure enough the light is coming from a small cottage nestled between two hills. You can't believe your luck. You pound on the door.

"Anyone home?" you call. No one comes to the door, so you peer through the frosty windows. Although the lights are on, the cottage is empty. The door is unlocked.

Inside you find a room with a large bed. The exhausted dogs jump onto the bed and settle down for a nap. You need to wait out the storm anyway, 101 so you join them. You huddle next to Sleepy and doze off.

TURN THE PAGE.

Suddenly you wake to someone shaking you. You blink your eyes.

"Snow-White?" you say surprised. "What are you doing here?"

"I got out of the weather station just in time and have been tracking your location," Snow-White explains. "I guess *I'm* the one saving *you*."

THE END

TO FOLLOW ANOTHER PATH, TURN TO PAGE 9.

103

You keep going, hoping you've made the right decision. You shake your fist in the air. "You can't stop me, Evil Queen!" you shout.

You can't feel your hands or feet. Your loyal dogs keep plunging through the snow and cold. Finally you see the weather station ahead – or at least where the weather station should be. In it's place is a huge mound of snow. You'll have to do a lot of digging to get Snow-White out.

With every bit of energy you have left, you claw at the snow. A shard of glass cuts through your glove and spots of red blood drop onto the white snow. With dread, you realize the glass walls of the weather station have collapsed under the weight of the snow.

Frantically you keep digging. At last you feel something. It is Snow-White's hand! You haul her out from under the snow.

Your friend is ice cold and isn't moving. You fear she's dead.

"No!" you scream. You kneel over her. Hot tears fall from your eyes onto her cold, blue face.

Suddenly you feel a cold hand touch your cheek. "It's OK," Snow-White's voice cuts into your sobs. "I'm alive."

You open your eyes, astonished. Snow-White slowly sits up and brushes the snow off her coat. Then she looks up at the sky. "Look!" she says. "The Evil Queen is gone."

You look up into a clear, cloudless sky. Light from the moon falls onto your face. You grin and hug Snow-White. You've survived the evil storm.

THE END

TO FOLLOW ANOTHER PATH, TURN TO PAGE 9.

CHAPTER 5

The many tales of Snow White

The story of Snow White was well known throughout Germany, even before it was published by brothers Jacob and Wilhelm Grimm. Researchers believe two sisters, Jeannette and Amalie Hassenpflug, told the Grimm brothers the story.

Although Snow White is a fairy tale, it may be based on actual events. Some people believe the story is based on the life of Margaretha von Waldeck, a 16th century German countess.

107

When Margaretha was 17 years old, she was sent away by her stepmother to live in Brussels, Belgium. There she fell in love with Prince Phillip II of Spain, and the two planned to marry. But Margaretha's parents disapproved of the relationship. Margaretha died mysteriously at age 21, possibly after being poisoned.

Others believe the story is based on Princess Maria Sophia Margaretha Catharina von Erthal, who was born in 1725. She lived in a castle in Lohr, Germany. Mirror manufacturers during this time made elaborate mirrors that were said to "always tell the truth". Some of these mirrors had small messages inscribed in the corners. Maria Sophia's father, Prince Phillip Christoph von Erthal, presented such a mirror to Claudia, his second wife. Claudia was a harsh stepmother, so Maria Sophia ran away to the forested mountains.

In the mountains, Maria Sophia came across miners from Bieber. Miners were often short and small so they could fit in narrow mining tunnels.

No one knows for certain if either story was the basis for Grimm's "Snow White and the Seven Dwarfs". But it's not just a German story. Hundreds of stories from Norway to Mozambique to Turkey to Italy tell similar tales. Although the stories are different, each one has a jealous parent or stepparent.

In 1937 Walt Disney produced an animated film called *Snow White and the Seven Dwarfs*. In his film Disney gave the dwarfs names: Happy, Grumpy, Sleepy, Sneezy, Dopey, Doc and Bashful. *Snow White and the Seven Dwarfs* was the first full-length animated Disney film. The film and the fairy tale are still loved today.

OTHER PATHS TO EXPLORE

1. This book tells three different stories featuring the character of Snow White. How might the stories be different if told from the perspective of the other characters, such as the dwarfs, the evil queen or the Huntsmen?

2. In the original fairy tale, the evil queen is jealous of Snow White and tries to harm her. Give an example of jealousy in one of the stories in this book.

3. Create your own version of *Snow White and the Seven Dwarfs*. Where does the story take place? Who are the characters?

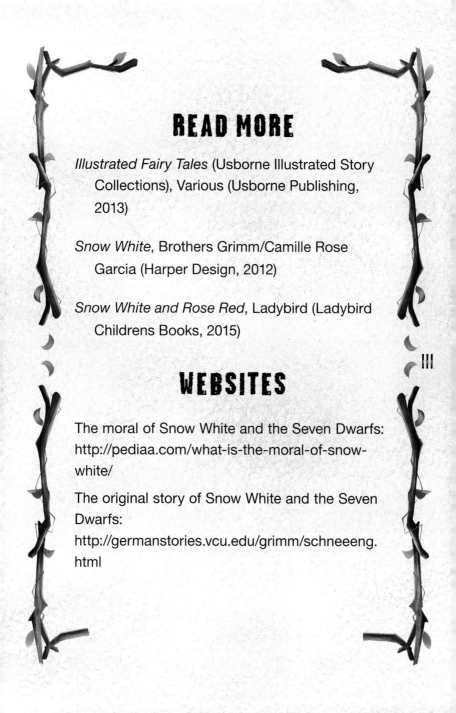

READ MORE

Illustrated Fairy Tales (Usborne Illustrated Story
Collections), Various (Usborne Publishing,
2013)

Snow White, Brothers Grimm/Camille Rose
Garcia (Harper Design, 2012)

Snow White and Rose Red, Ladybird (Ladybird
Childrens Books, 2015)

WEBSITES

The moral of Snow White and the Seven Dwarfs:
http://pediaa.com/what-is-the-moral-of-snow-
white/

The original story of Snow White and the Seven
Dwarfs:
http://germanstories.vcu.edu/grimm/schneeeng.
html

LOOK FOR ALL THE BOOKS
IN THIS SERIES:

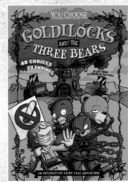

Rediscovering Europe

Other publications available from Demos

Making Europe popular: the search for European identity
EuroVisions: new dimensions of European integration
Politics without frontiers: the role of political parties in Europe's future
The post-modern state and the world order
Britain™: renewing our identity

To order a publication or a free catalogue please contact Demos

Publications available from Interbrand Newell and Sorrell

The trouble with words
The secret of design effectiveness
A–W: a directory of recent work
Power-packed (design effectiveness paper no 1)
Books: the great escape (design effectiveness paper no 2)
Brands — the new wealth creators
Trademark law
Brand valuation
The world's greatest brands

To order any of these publications please contact Interbrand Newell and Sorrell

DEM☉S

Demos is an independent think tank committed to radical thinking on the long-term problems facing the UK and other advanced industrial societies.

It aims to develop ideas – both theoretical and practical – to help shape the politics of the twenty first century, and to improve the breadth and quality of political debate.

Demos publishes books and a regular journal and undertakes substantial empirical and policy oriented research projects. Demos is a registered charity.

In all its work, Demos brings together people from a wide range of backgrounds in business, academia, government, the voluntary sector and the media to share and cross-fertilise ideas and experiences.

For further information and subscription details please contact:
Demos, 9 Bridewell Place, London EC4V 6AP
Tel + 44 (0) 171 353 4479   Fax + 44 (0) 171 353 4481
e-mail: mail@demos.co.uk

Interbrand Newell and Sorrell

Interbrand Newell and Sorrell is part of the Interbrand Group, the world's leading branding and identity business. Working across the world in 17 countries the company is dedicated to building brand and corporate value for it's clients, helping them to create, develop, manage, sustain and value their corporate, product and service brands and identities.

For further information please contact:
Amber Collins, Interbrand Newell and Sorrell, 4 Utopia Village,
Chalcot Road, London NW1 8LH
Tel + 44 (0) 171 722 1113   Fax + 44 (0) 171 722 0259
e-mail: n+s@inspire-me.com

Rediscovering Europe

Mark Leonard

in association with

Interbrand Newell and Sorrell

First published in 1998
by Demos
9 Bridewell Place
London EC4V 6AP

ISBN 1 898309 54 X

Printed in Great Britain by
Spin Offset

Design by
Interbrand Newell and Sorrell

Contents

Acknowledgements

I am most grateful to Interbrand Newell and Sorrell for funding the research that went into this report, and in particular to Frances Newell, John Sorrell, Lynne Dobney, Tony Allen, John Simmons, David Carroll, Caroline Wilson, Peggy Connor and Rob Finlay for their support, advice and assistance.

I warmly thank my research team Kay Chung and Tilo Fuchs, without whose hard work, shrewd insights and dogged persistence this volume would not have been possible. I must thank Geoff Mulgan, Ian Christie and Perri 6 for their ideas, their patient support, their time and their comments on successive drafts. I would also like to thank Debbie Porter, George Lawson, Tom Hampson, Tom Bentley, Ben Jupp, Siân Gibson, Richard Warner, Lindsay Nash and Kendra Pearce at Demos for ideas, inspiration, practical assistance and, above all, for putting up with me as I approached my final deadline.

Very special thanks must go to Phillip Dodd for his unstinting support, radical ideas and generosity in hosting lunches and launches at the ICA. I am extremely grateful to Shaun Riordan and the British Embassy in Spain for immense hospitality and kindness, and for bringing together some of the finest minds in Spain at such short notice. I am indebted to Christine Gamble and Roger Budd at the British Council in Paris for being such wonderful hosts at the Paris seminar. I also thank Guillaume McGlaughlin, John Palmer, Rolf Gustavsson and Stanley Crossick at the European Policy Centre for organising and hosting a very successful seminar in Brussels. Special thanks also go to Robert Cooper at the British Embassy in Bonn for his insightful comments, and his skillful chairing of the Hamburg seminar. I should also thank Soren Steen Olsen, for inviting me to lead two very fruitful discussions at the Institute for Future Studies in Copenhagen. Special thanks also go to Simon Hix at the LSE for advice, inspiration and valuable data. I must also warmly thank Geoffrey Edwards for his comments on an earlier draft and for teaching me much of what I know about the EU. I am grateful to Alison Hook and the London office of the European Commission for information, support and advice on the project.

The ideas that went into this volume were the product of an extensive programme of interviews and focus sessions right across Europe. During this process many people provided invaluable help by allowing me to interview them, coming to seminars and providing me with practical assistance and data. It is impossible to name everyone who helped, but these are some of the most deserving of thanks: Danny Alexander, European Movement; Duka Arangurren, Fundacíon Pablo Iglesias; Simon Atkinson, Mori; Jose Maria de Arielza Carvajal, Gabinete de la Presidencia del Gobierno; Bertrand Badre, Ministère des Finances; Franck Biancheri, Prometheus-Europe; Barbara Bicknell, INJEP; Lissa Bradley, Nôtre Europe; Dr Juergen Brautmeier, Landesanstalt fur Rundfunk NRW; Dr Emanuele Castano, Université Catholique de Louvain; Dr Valerie Caton, British Embassy, Paris; Gilles Corman, SOFRES; Ignacio Cosido, Guardia Civil; John Crowley, CERI; Professor Norman Davies, Wolfson College, Oxford; Frederic Delouche, Groupe des Belles Feuilles; Peter Dunn, Foreign and Commonwealth Office; Gabriele Eick, Konzernstab Kommunikation; Alberto Elordi, Fundacíon Alternativas; Lucia Extebarria; John Fitzmaurice, European Commission; Manuel Florentin; Tony Fretton; Timothy Garton Ash, St Anthony's College, Oxford; Dr Rainer M Giersch, RCN Marketing Consultants Network; Professor Paul

Gilroy, Goldsmiths College, London; Charles Grant, Centre for European Reform; Gabriel Guallard, Sciences Politiques; Philip Gumuchdjian, Richard Rogers Partnership; Professor Peter Hall, Bartlett School of Planning, University College London; Charles Hampden-Turner, Judge Institute of Management Studies, Cambridge; Ian Hargreaves; David Harrisson; Uwe Hasebrink, Institut fur Medien-forschung; Chris Haskins; Gordon Heald, ORB; Professor Eric Hobsbawm, Birkbeck College, London; Michael Horsham, Tomato; Esteban Ibarra, Jovenes Contra la Intolerancia; Professeur Pièrre Iselin, Paris III; Paul Jaeger, Sources d'Europe; Pierre Jaillard, Jeunes Fonctionnaires Européens; Martin Jacques; Thomas Jansen, European Commission; Janice Kirkpatrick, Graven Images; Francois Laquièze, mission pour la célébration de l'an 2000; Matthew Laza, Labour Movement for Europe; Charlie Leadbeater, European Movement; Jo Leadbeater, European Movement; Sharon Leclerq-Spooner, Club 2020; Robert Leicht, Die Zeit; Mariot Leslie, Foreign and Commonwealth Office; John Lloyd, New Statesman; Catherine Laurent, Editions Didier; Marcel Loko, Zum Goldenen Hirschen; Adam Lury, Howell Henry Chaldecott and Lury; Catherine Marcangeli, Paris VII; Anna Mellich, European Commission; Professor David Morely, Goldsmiths College, London; Linda Myles, Pandora Productions; Luis Ortega, Fundacíon Pablo Iglesias; Karlheinz Reif, European Commission; Richard Rogers, Richard Rogers Partnership; Andrea Rose, British Council; Sabine Rosenblatt, Die Woche; Marie-Luce Ribôt, Sud Ouest; Dr Felipé Sahagun; Jean-Claude Sérgeant, Paris III; José Felix Tezanos, Fundacíon Sistema; Nathalie Tousignant, Université Catholoique de Louvain; Patrice Vivancos, Forum Film Européen; Françoise de la Serre, CERI; Chris Shore, Goldsmith's College, London; Professor Anthony D Smith, LSE; César Vidal; Phillipe Ward, Rothschild & Cie; Andrew Warren, Cap Gemini; Stephen Woodard, European Movement.

I must also thank Amber Collins and Annabel Purves at Interbrand Newell and Sorrell for organising and analysing our poll of business leaders. During the course of the research I have been given privileged access to sources of opinion data, both published and unpublished. I would like to thank in particular the European Movement, MORI, the European Values Group, Eurobarometer, Synergy, Opinion Research Business, The Henley Centre, EUROPINION and British Social Attitudes.

Finally, I would like to thank my sister Miriam Leonard and my parents Dick and Iréne Leonard for being so wonderful. This volume is dedicated to them.

Mark Leonard, June 1998

Introduction: a tale of two Europes

On the eve of its most ambitious projects to date – Economic and Monetary Union (EMU) and enlargement – the European Union (EU) is less popular than it has been for a generation. Despite its many successes, it often appears to the public to be a secretive bureaucracy that spends its time laying down impenetrable regulations, operating behind closed doors.

The paradox is that in other ways Europe is stronger than ever. It is more integrated in its concerns, more visible and present in our everyday lives, in the new jobs we do, the companies we deal with, the food we eat, the places we travel to, the values, cultures and priorities we share.

Yet the EU has not succeeded in turning this latent 'Europeanism' into popular support for European integration. The problem is that the EU's leaders have tended to think about the issue of legitimacy in the wrong way and to look for it in the wrong places. In the past, there were two general ways of thinking about the EU's legitimacy problems. One approach saw the EU's unpopularity as a product of either having 'too much' or 'too little' integration. The Eurosceptic response was to argue for 'less EU' by repatriating powers to member states. The pro-European response was to make Europe more like a nation state, by building federal institutions like the European Parliament, establishing European citizenship or creating symbols and an identity on the national model. The other approach has been to pin Europe's legitimacy problems on an information deficit. Many have argued that if the public were only made more aware of what the EU is doing – and if the Commission had a better information strategy – the EU would become more popular.

This pamphlet calls for a new approach to the question of legitimacy. It argues that those who believe that the project of integration in Europe is inherently unpopular and doomed to fail are wrong; there is in fact strong latent support across the member states and beyond for further European integration. But it also rejects the conventional solutions to Europe's legitimacy problems. The view that Europe can be made more popular through institutional innovations alone – or recreating the nation state at a higher level – has over the years proved ineffectual. And those who believe that Europe's key problem is simply one of communication, one that could be solved by bigger information campaigns, a new flag or better advertising, are equally wrong.

In fact, the EU is unpopular not because we have the wrong 'amount' of European integration, or because people aren't informed about the project of ever closer union in the right way, but because we have the wrong kind of European Union. In short, the EU is unpopular because its institutions and preoccupations have become detached from its people.

There are four core elements to this. First, the EU has become detached from people's everyday experience of Europe. As a result of greater mobility and convergence of consumption, people have a growing sense of Europe as a continent and an emerging 'European' identity.[1] But, as yet, most Europeans do not identify the EU with their idea of Europe, and the EU has failed to embody it.

Secondly, the EU's institutional priorities do not fit well with the priorities of its people. While Europe's voters are primarily concerned with key dimensions of quality of life – the availability and quality of jobs, fear of crime and the state of the natural and built environment – Europe's leaders devote most of their time and money to EMU and the Common Agricultural Policy (CAP).[2]

Thirdly, the EU has not succeeded in spreading the benefits of EU membership. From early on most of the direct benefits have gone to minority groups and areas – farmers, declining industries and underdeveloped regions. Since the single market most of the indirect benefits have been felt by the better educated and more mobile. The result is that many people don't feel they have benefited – the EU is seen as 'Club-class'.[3]

Finally, the EU has lost its sense of mission and is not fully geared up to meet the major challenges of the future. Its core mission, priorities and purpose have not been reinvented since the end of the Cold War, which shaped so many of the old Community's priorities. Each of the original missions of peace, prosperity and democracy has lost force. In their place there is nothing capable of inspiring European citizens – even historic moves towards enlargement and EMU have become embroiled in technical wrangles. European leaders appear to lack a compelling vision for the future beyond vague aspirations to create a Union which has superpower status in the global economy and political order.[4]

This situation is largely a product of success. What seemed half a century ago to be an improbable vision has been achieved: war in western Europe is unthinkable, prosperity has spread throughout the EU states to a degree unimaginable in the 1950s, and the Union has established a set of institutions for collaboration and consensus-building between interdependent states that is unique.[5] But today we need to recognise that the European order has changed fundamentally since the 1950s – especially since 1989.

The challenge is to rediscover what it means to be European and to think afresh about the next phase of European integration – for the next 40 years. That is what this pamphlet is about: building a Europe that is based on the priorities, values and lifestyles of European citizens and is ready to deal with the economic, environmental and social challenges we all face.

Over the past six months we have conducted expert seminars, focus group discussions, in-depth interviews and

'What Europe needs is a new narrative that describes a new reality. But instead it has a jungle of decision-making that people don't understand. It has become clear that simply reforming institutions is not enough to produce legitimacy'. *Rudolf Scharping, SPD*

opinion surveys across Europe to find out what people from all over the continent think being European is about, and what they want from the project of European integration in the future. The result is this report. We have distilled the data and analysis to develop seven 'narratives' which could be used to help form the basis of a new European identity and provide a sense of direction for the next phase of European integration. Each one is about rediscovering what Europe is for and what it means to its citizens. They are positive and bold aims for the future – mission statements for a real people's Europe.

Detached institutions:
why the European project is unpopular

Four decades after its inception, the EU's very right to exist is still being debated in many European countries. Fewer than half of Europeans think their country's membership of the EU is a good thing, and only four out of ten think that their country benefits from EU membership.[6] These results make dismal reading for supporters of European integration, on the eve of Europe's most ambitious developments yet. But they are not altogether surprising.

In order to understand where we are today, we must understand how we got here. In a very real sense, the legitimacy problems of today are the direct result of the past 40 years of European integration.

European integration was about performing seemingly impossible tasks: regenerating the European economy, bringing peace to a continent more used to the ravages of war and establishing democracy in countries with authoritarian traditions and recent experience of vicious totalitarianism. In many ways, the EU was about saving European publics and politicians from themselves. It was born in an era when public approval mattered relatively little and when the wider geo-political agenda was utterly dominated by the Cold War. Its concerns were technocratic and so were its means – the more depoliticised it could be, the better. Claude Cheysson, a former French foreign minister and European commissioner, is on record as saying that 'Europe could only be created in the absence of democracy'.

While the memory and fear of war were strong, and while economic recovery dominated popular concerns, it was possible for the European project to be an elite enterprise, a benign technocratic conspiracy designed to bring about irreversible integration. A 'permissive consensus' allowed national governments to take decisions about European integration without any real popular mandate. Even today, throughout the EU, the public sees European integration as 'inevitable' – even when they disagree with it. So although across Europe only 53 per cent say they support the introduction of the single currency, and more than half 'fear' its introduction, three out of four people expect it to happen regardless.[7]

When the EU was only concerned with providing common standards for tomato paste composition or lawn-mower sound emissions, this model of technocratic 'integration for your own good' was sustainable. But today, with the end of the Cold War and the rise of an EU that is responsible for half of all domestic legislation and 80 per cent of economic and social legislation, the situation has changed utterly.[8] Now that most of the technical issues (product standards, mutual recognition of education certificates and so on) have been settled, the European agenda is increasingly dominated by more contentious and salient issues. The decisions taken over convergence criteria laid down at Maastricht and over working conditions have direct a impact on people's lives and welfare. What is more, the twin projects of EMU and enlargement will transform the nature of the EU and place new burdens on EU citizens and budgets.

The main reason that the EU often inspires suspicion, fear or cynicism among many citizens across the member states is that during the course of 40 years of technocratic integration, it has become accustomed to being detached from its citizens. This poses four major problems for the legitimacy of the EU project. Firstly, the EU does not embody the things that most people associate with the continent of Europe, or foster a positive sense of identification with its goals and structures; secondly, its priorities do not appear to reflect citizens' key concerns and aspirations for the future; thirdly, it has been unable to demonstrably shed it's 'club-class' image and spread tangible benefits to a majority, rather than concentrating on farmers, underdeveloped regions, and those with high skills, and high incomes who benefit most from the single market; finally, it has no convincing vision of where it is going and how it is planning to meet the strategic challenges facing Europe over the longer term.

People feel part of Europe but not the EU

The first problem is that although many people increasingly feel 'European' as well as a member of a nation or region or other grouping, they do not identify positively with the EU.

Exactly half of EU citizens feel that they will develop a European component to their identity 'in the near future'[9]. One in ten see their European identity as stronger than their national identity.[10] And, if you separate European identity from national identity more explicitly and ask 'in addition to your own sense of nationality, how European do you feel?', respondents give replies that are even more positive. Two thirds of UK citizens claim to feel 'European', with this formulation.[11]

Yet when pollsters ask those who claim to feel 'European' what this means to them, they tend not to mention the EU. Focus group research work has indicated that people find it difficult to give a definite meaning to 'being European' – they might associate it with culture, history, a shared geographical space, travelling, food and a set of values. Above all, they say that it is something they might feel if confronted with, say, Japanese or American people. But they are unlikely to link a feeling of belonging to Europe to their nation's membership of the EU. Ironically, people are more likely to identify with

'The key to being European is a sense of innovation and creativity. The problem with European institutions is that they don't have a clear defining mission. They have no big ideas and creativity – they are just grey and dull.' *Adam Lury, Howell, Henry, Chaldcott and Lury*

Europe if they come from countries outside the EU. In a recent survey, 59 per cent of Poles and 42 per cent of Czechs claimed that their European identity was as strong as their national identity – a far higher proportion than any of the EU countries covered in the same poll.[12]

'The invasion of European football players is seen by most people as a good thing. Ordinary kids in Britain will follow their favourite players around Europe and say 'my team is Juventus'.
Martin Jacques

'Greeks and Italians experience Europe through their diaspora. They have become the caterers of Europe – every European city has their restaurants.'
John Lloyd,
The New Statesman

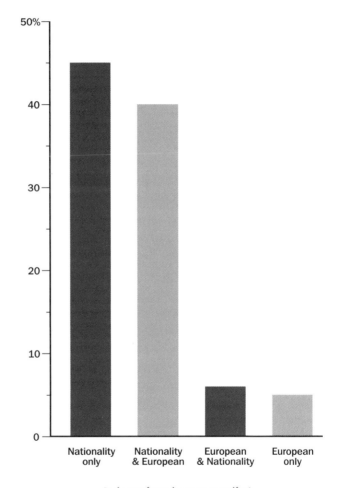

In the near future do you see yourself as?

It is important not to overstate this reported sense of identity. As many as 45 per cent of EU citizens say that they do not feel any kind of European identity, and there are structural barriers to its development.[13] The linguistic diversity of the Union is the major block to any notion of integration on the lines of the USA. The fact that over half of Europeans are incapable of having a conversation in a second language has made the development of a common media and cultural life impossible so far.[14] It has also seriously hampered labour mobility. Fewer than one in 50 (1.6 per cent) EU citizens is resident in another EU country.[15] Even Belgium, the only country with a significant number of EU nationals from different countries living in it, has only 5 per cent.[16]

Despite this, there is evidence of a gradual emergence of a common culture. There is increasing convergence at the micro-social level in Europe: as affluence grows, so consumers develop tastes, priorities and concerns in common, and more people become accustomed to travelling around the continent for business or leisure.[17] Household structures and family patterns are becoming similar, albeit slowly, with Mediterranean trends beginning to follow North European developments.[18] Economic integration exposes more people across the Union to similar working practices, problems and opportunities.

The fragments of this emerging European cultural identity and lifestyle are stored away in holiday snapshots and memories of art, literature, music, buildings and landscape. It is a product of people's ability to experience Europe directly – unmediated by national governments and European institutions. The process has been accelerated by things that have brought about everyday Europeanism: cheaper travel, Inter-rail, the Channel Tunnel, the growth of European restaurants, and European food on supermarket shelves, the Eurovision Song Contest, the ERASMUS exchange programme, the relaxation of border of controls, European sporting contests, Euronews, etc. The international

'Europeans will start identifying with the EU when the EU delivers outcomes that they want'.
John Fitzmaurice, European Commission

'When the Euro-rail generation think Europe they see 'Europe espace' not 'Europe puissance'. They don't see it as a project and they don't know about national history'.
Professor William Wallace, London School of Economics

make-up of football teams is another of the many forces acclimatising people to a sense of 'being European' which overlaps with, rather than takes over from, other identities at national, regional or local level. Footballers such as Ruud Gullit and Jürgen Klinsmann (and other French, Dutch, Italian or German players in the English Premiership) embody an attractive mingling of local, national and Euro-identities whose influences is far-reaching. As the social theorist Manuel Castells points out: 'It is through this kind of basic life mechanisms that the real Europe is coming into existence – by sharing experience on the basis of meaningful palpable identity'.[19] For all the linguistic and cultural barriers to integration, this nascent 'European identity' is real.

So why don't people associate it with the EU? The first reason that people don't feel part of the EU is that they have not been part of its construction. It was brought about behind closed doors in chancelleries and conference centres by policy elites. The other reason is that the EU has failed to embody many of the things people associate with 'being European' and has not harnessed the forces for micro-social integration.

This matters because political systems cannot just rely on support for day-to-day activities in the good times, they need to be given the benefit of the doubt in the bad times as well. This means fostering a sense of identity which allows governments to take 'tough decisions' or bring about major change without the existence of the whole political system being called into question. As the EU embarks on the potentially disruptive and high-risk experiment of EMU and faces the challenges of enlargement, it needs more than a new version of the 'permissive consensus' of the earlier phases of integration. It needs people to feel part of it.

Disconnected: the mismatch between EU priorities and citizens' concerns

The second problem is that the EU has not based European integration on the ambitions and aspirations of its citizens. It is ironic that, at a time when other political systems are putting increasing resources into monitoring shifts in the priorities and values of their citizens, the EU's operational priorities should be so far removed from the priorities of its citizens.

Although EU citizens know little about the EU's structures and processes, they have no such doubts about what it should be doing. Opinion surveys have consistently shown their priorities. Ninety two per cent see 'fighting unemployment' as a priority; 89 per cent say the same about 'fighting poverty and social exclusion'; 88 per cent about 'maintaining peace and security' in Europe; and 85 per cent about 'protecting the environment'.[20]

The EU, by contrast, devotes most of its time and budget to issues that are not seen as priorities. Only one in ten (9 per cent) Europeans see 'ensuring an adequate income for farmers' as important, but half the EU budget and one fifth of ministerial meetings are devoted to the Common Agricultural Policy. The same small percentage sees EMU as a priority, yet more time is spent on this than any other policy area. Only 46 per cent see 'reforming the institutions of the EU and the way they work' as a priority, yet these activities play a large part in the EU's public communications.[21]

There is a gulf developing between European decision-makers and European citizens. A recent survey in the UK showed that only 15 per cent thought that the EU was 'in touch with people'.[22] Another poll has revealed the difference between the attitudes to Europe of 'top decision-makers' (politicians, high level civil servants, business and labour leaders, the media and leading players in academic, cultural and religious life) and 'ordinary' citizens. Ninety four per cent of decision-makers thought their country's

'How can we justify monetary union in Europe to our citizens if we are not even capable of dealing with the outbreak of a war in the middle of Europe?'
Wolfgang Schäuble, CDU

membership of the EU was a good thing – compared to 48 per cent of ordinary citizens.[23] Nine out of ten thought their country benefited from EU membership, compared to 42 per cent of ordinary people.[24] Eighty five per cent were in favour of EMU compared to 51 per cent of the general public.[25]

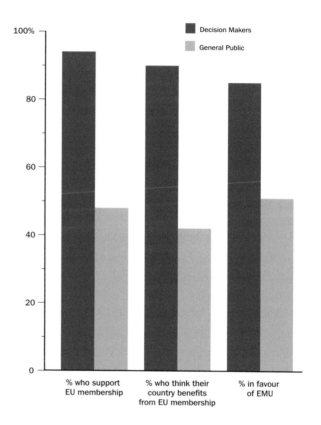

The gulf between decision-makers and the public

One of the clearest indicators of this is the difference in the public's reactions to the Amsterdam Treaty and the Luxembourg employment summit. Although the Amsterdam Treaty marked the end of the Inter-Governmental Conference (IGC) and signified major institutional change – including a large extension of the European Parliament's power – only one third of EU citizens (34 per cent) said

'The development of the EU was only possible in the absence of democracy. The idea that there is a 'democratic deficit' is absurd as it assumes that democracy was part of the original equation. The EU was never intended to be democratic'.
Professor Eric Hobsbawm, Birbeck College, London

24   *Rediscovering Europe*

that they knew about it.[26] Yet the employment summit, which took place a few months later and made no real substantive decisions, was noticed by 55 per cent of European citizens.[27] There is no question that more energy was put into Amsterdam by European decision-makers, but the fact that the Luxembourg summit was seen to be dealing with issues that related to most people's priorities rather than the vagaries of institutional reform made it far more memorable.

The public's response to the inability of European Union institutions and activities to make a genuine priority of their concerns has been apathy on a grand scale. Turnout in European parliamentary elections has consistently been lower than in national elections in all member states and has fallen with each succeeding election (in the UK it hit an unimpressive glass ceiling of 36.5 per cent). There are a variety of explanations for the low turnout in the Europe elections, but this gap between what the public wants from Europe and what it gets must be a major part of any diagnosis.

'For people over 35 the fundamental idea of Europe is democracy, intertwined with a vague idea of common culture. For under 35s there is no clear idea at all.'
José-Felix Tezano, Fundacíon Sistema

Club-class Europe: the failure to spread the benefits of EU membership

The third problem is the EU's failure to deliver tangible benefits to a majority of its citizens.

One problem is that, people rarely experience 'the EU' directly as most of its actions are mediated by national or local government. In fact, 97 per cent of Europeans say that they have never had any direct contact with the EU.[28] This is coupled with the fact that national and local governments are happy to take credit for popular measures and, conversely, have no qualms about letting the EU take the blame for unpopular ones.

Even with that caveat, it is clear that the EU has not succeeded in spreading the benefits of membership as widely as it might. From early on, most of the direct benefits of EU membership have been enjoyed by minority groups and areas – farmers, heavy industry and residents of underdeveloped regions. Some of these measures played a part in fostering social inclusion across member states and mitigating the worst effects of industrial decline, but there is a colossal lack of proportion. Though today almost half of EU citizens live in areas that are entitled to money from the European Union structural funds, the amounts involved pale into insignificance when compared with the 48 per cent of the budget that is devoted to farmers. They represent only 6.5 per cent of EU citizens, and generate less than 3 per cent of EU GDP, half the EU budget is devoted to farm subsidies, and many of these payments go to support activities of low social value with undesirable impacts on the environment.

Most of the economic benefits that flow from EU membership – particularly since the creation of the single market – are indirect. But these are also unevenly spread. They are most likely to be felt by those in managerial and professional areas with high skills and high incomes, or such as students who are more mobile. Research shows that these people are much more likely to support European Integration, and to think that their country has benefited from EU membership.

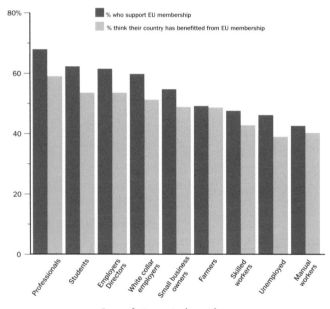

■ % who support EU membership
□ % think their country has benefitted from EU membership

Support for integration by social group

In fact, in each occupational group – other than manual workers – reported feelings of having gained benefits from the EU rise with income. Increasingly, there is a division between the affluent and successful and the less secure employees and traders, between the Europe of the powerful and the powerless. And in Britain, only one in four thinks that the EU has a good record at 'raising the standard of living for ordinary people', compared to 38 per cent who think it has a poor record.

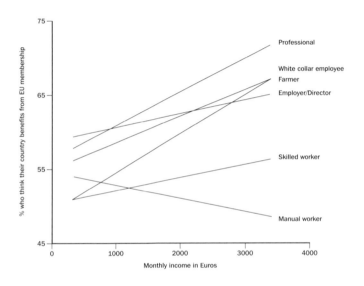

Feelings of benefit from EU according to income and social group

The link between economic insecurity and wider problems of legitimacy for the EU is evident from the data on support for integration. Many commentators interpret the current legitimacy problems as a consequence of Maastricht, but in fact positive responses to survey questions about support for the EU peaked by the autumn of 1990. Karlheinz Reif argues that 'as sectoral discussions about the specific issues of "1992" became visible, general approval, and even more clearly, hope in the single market, began to decline.

People no longer felt they were being asked to react to the European project in the abstract, but were now responding to specific issues as they affected their everyday lives and were ranking their priorities accordingly.'[29] The economic turbulence of the 1990s and the uneven consequences for quality of life that have flowed from recession, the single market, deregulation and the wave of mergers and acquisitions across the EU have had an important impact on popular perceptions of what the Union can do for the average citizen, and how far its concerns are those of the general public.[30]

The EU in search of a mission: facing up to the strategic challenges to Europe

The most serious problem for the Union, however, is that EU leaders have failed to develop a convincing vision for the future of Europe – one that deals with the strategic challenges ahead and offers a compelling 'narrative' of what further integration is actually for.

Today, Europe is in the midst of a profound change. The impact of the external pressures of globalisation and the end of the Cold War have changed the geo-political and economic environment. There are external security pressures from the east and south – migration, military and environmental. Economic competition from Asia in particular has intensified and requires faster restructuring by European industries. At the same time, the twin projects of EMU and enlargement will transform the nature of the EU, as well as placing new burdens of EU citizens and budgets. What is more, they come hot on the heels of changes to the EU which have made it responsible for half of all domestic legislation and 80 per cent of economic and social legislation across the member states.

Many people will support a regime that has a clear sense of direction, even if they disagree with specific policy decisions. But without one there is always a danger of being buffeted by events.

Faced with these challenges, EU leaders have been unsure and unconvincing. They have, in the eyes of their citizens, lost this clear sense of mission. Peace, prosperity and democracy – the compelling clarion calls which motivated the foundation of what is now the Union – have each lost much of their resonance. They are still the key reasons why the countries of central and eastern Europe want to join – but within the EU they have lost their purchase.

Peace is taken for granted by a generation in western Europe that has never known war. In a recent survey fewer than one in four fifteen to 24 year olds cited 'peace' when asked what the EU meant to them personally.[31] Despite various attempts by Helmut Kohl and other politicians to claim that further integration is 'a matter of peace or war', many people feel the opposite, particularly in view of the EU's inability to prevent the bloody fiasco of Yugoslavia's break-up. The guarantee of prosperity has been tarnished by burgeoning unemployment and economic insecurity. In fact, many people have come to blame the EU and the Maastricht convergence criteria for their economic difficulties. And the EU's role as guardian and promoter of democracy has been constrained and damaged by its complex and opaque decision-making system. In fact, many people – particularly in the UK – even see the EU leeching away national democracy, without creating a credible supranational substitute.

These elements of the European mission need to be updated, enriched and supplemented by new narratives of what integration is intended to do for Europeans. At present, European leaders have little to offer beyond vague aspirations of building a European superpower or superstate. Even the historic enlargement to the east and the project of Economic and Monetary Union have become embroiled in technical wranglings, and there is no longer a clear sense of what the EU is embarking on these grandiose projects for. Part of the problem is that for years the sole mission of European integration has been 'ever-closer Union', which

'European leaders could have made enlargement into an exciting common project – instead they have reduced it to a series of technical wrangles. The same has happened with foreign and security policy.'
Professor William Wallace, London School of Economics

begs the question 'for what?'. Europe's leaders have failed to realise that if the debate continues to be conducted solely in terms of 'more Europe versus less Europe', they are in danger of ending up with a substantial proportion of the public seeing no purpose for 'Europe' at all.

Because there is no sense of direction on the strategic issues, many Europeans have lost faith in the ability of European institutions to deliver. The high profile given to fraud and waste and the costs of the Common Agricultural Policy, coupled with the visible failure of important EU initiatives such as its attempts to intervene in the former Yugoslavia, have dealt serious blows to the EU's image – making Europeans increasingly sceptical about the efficacy of European institutions.

Only one in three (36 per cent) think that they can 'rely on' European institutions – a drop of 6 per cent in the last two years.[32] They are even sceptical about the EU's performance at its foundation roles. For example, only half of UK citizens think the EU has a good record at 'bringing peace to Europe since the second world war', while as many as 22 per cent think it has a bad one.[33]

This matters because when there is no sense of an attractive 'Big picture', support for the process of European integration becomes closely linked to the fate of particular policies. Whereas a national political system does not usually run into trouble when a government policy is disliked (it will at most result in the election of a new government), the EU as a whole comes under fire and is at risk of legitimacy crises if a particular policy is perceived to be ineffective or wasteful. This underlines the risk that is being run in the establishment of EMU when public opinion has evidently not been sufficiently prepared or won over to the project. It also shows the need for individual policies to be linked to a bigger picture, if they are going to attract the interest and support of EU citizens.

Things can get better

The good news is that survey data and qualitative evidence show that levels of both support and opposition to the EU are very shallow.[34] As Karlheinz Reif, a former head of the EU's polling wing, points out: 'the EU has neither attracted enthusiastic support nor explicit opposition'. In fact, even in the 1997 general election in Britain, when Europe had dominated the campaign, it was never one of the top issues for voters.[35]

So, in the absence of major policy triumphs or disasters, most people do not feel strongly either way about EU membership and are willing to be swayed by positive experience. Even in the UK, survey evidence indicates that a majority would be prepared to trade a loss in economic sovereignty in return for higher living standards.[36] This suggests that if the EU is seen to relate to people's priorities and values and is seen to deliver tangible benefits to its citizens, as well as having a clear sense of direction, it could go a long way to solving its legitimacy problems.

'Continents that play together stay together. It's time for a European football team!'
John Lloyd, New Statesman

Why the existing attempts to build legitimacy will not work

There have been many attempts by supporters of European integration to tackle the EU's legitimacy problems. First, they have tried to use the techniques that originally legitimised nation states in order to make the EU more popular. The second approach has been to treat the EU's unpopularity as a lack of information and to look for communication strategies to fill this deficit.

Replicating the national model

Many have argued that to become popular, the EU must simply push integration deeper and adopt the techniques that were used to build and legitimate the nation state. In doing this, they have focused on three areas: reforming institutions to make them more democratic, creating a notion of European citizenship and building a political identity for Europeans.

Institution-building

First, many have argued for building 'federalist' institutions to reduce the 'democratic deficit'. The most commonly proposed solution is giving greater powers to the European

Parliament. But given the lack of enthusiasm for voting in Euro-elections, this strategy is problematic. A recent qualitative survey by MORI found that 'familiarity with institutions such as the European Parliament is almost non-existent'.[37] In any case, European elections are at present more likely to serve as a protest against national governments than as a genuine expression of opinion on common European issues. Furthermore, as European parliamentary elections will lead to the formation of neither a government nor a coherent programme of public policy – the two key functions of democratic elections – they are even less likely to give the EU greater legitimacy.

Other innovations which have been mooted include televising parts of the European Council and Council of Ministers' meetings, giving national parliaments a bigger role in European decision-making, and even holding direct elections for the president of the Commission.

While all of these measures might be positive in their own right, they are unlikely, on their own, to make the European project more popular. There is no reason to suppose that enhanced access to the transcripts of a meeting on food standards, or the chance to watch fisheries ministers battling it out over mesh sizes on television, or for that matter more grandstanding by leading politicians, would increase public satisfaction with the EU. In fact it is quite possible that it would result in even greater public apathy. And in practice they are not likely to happen in the near future; most of these ideas have been discussed for some time without being implemented.

Above all, if turnout continues to fall in many national and local elections and the key source of people's identity continues to shift from the level of political institutions and principles to that of more localised associational practices, lifestyles and emotional ties with family and friends, it seems unlikely that political institution-building will greatly affect the EU's standing with its citizens.[38]

'We need to create a new kind of citizenship. A European social contract that confers real rights and responsibilities that don't already exist at a national level. People will need to have European duties and voluntary service, and be willing to pay taxes.'
Jose Maria de Arielza Carvajal, Gabinete de la Presidencia del Gobierno

Citizenship

Many have argued that one of the main sources of legitimacy for the nation state is the citizenship rights that it affords
to its residents. Attempts have therefore been made to shift
these benefits to a European level. The introduction of citizenship of the Union in the Maastricht treaty gives natu-
ralised citizens in any member states the right to move and
reside freely within the territory of the Community; to vote
and be eligible to stand in local and Euro-elections; to for-
mulate a petition to the European Parliament; to apply to a
Union ombudsman; and to have consular representation in
non-member states where one's own country does not have
a consulate.

But this approach misunderstands the role of citizenship
in nation states. Citizenship played a powerful role in creating national identity and legitimating the state at a national
level because it offered definite and concrete benefits to the
people to whom it was extended: greater freedoms, material
security and access to new institutions. People were given
protection and rights that they badly wanted: human and
civil rights (which are safeguarded by the European
Council, not the EU); political rights (which on the EU level
simply lack a meaningful forum – that is, a European government); and social rights embodied in the welfare state
(which are not part of the EU treaties and are not on the
integrationist agenda for the foreseeable future). This severe-
ly limits the scope for possible benefits attached to 'EU citizenship'.

As a result, much of the European integration debate is
not so much about affording new rights to individuals as
repackaging existing rights with a European gloss (the relevant article in the Maastricht treaty even makes it clear that
EU citizenship is tied to national citizenship and does not
have a basis of its own). Moreover, although the new rights
that are guaranteed by European citizenship, (such as voting
in other countries or joint recognition of qualifications), are
vital to promote labour market mobility, they only offer

concrete benefits to the 1.6 per cent of EU citizens who live in other countries. And, in fact, only one in four Europeans is interested in being able 'to vote or stand as a candidate in local elections or European elections' if they are resident in another country, while 63 per cent say that they are not interested.[39]

But even if one ignores these problems, the very word 'citizenship' has its limitations as it has very different meanings in different EU countries. In English it is a neutral word, without the power to enthuse. In France it has revolutionary connotations, allying it very firmly with the past, rather than the future. In eastern Europe, it has very negative associations, linked to the jargon used by police and other authorities in the communist era. Only in Italy is it seen as a positive word that people like to use to describe themselves and the roles they play. But even in Italy, polling evidence suggests that people are more likely to describe themselves as 'citizens of the world' than 'citizens of the European Union'.[40]

If European citizenship is going to work, it has to prove that it is giving the majority of people something they need and something they cannot get at a national level. Citizenship will only acquire meaning when it translates into real entitlements.

'The added benefits of citizenship are predicated on people moving around. But most people don't move around, they need to develop an identity where they are now.'
John Fitzmaurice, European Commission

Building an identity

Finally, they have sought to build an identity on the nation state model. This became a focus of Euro-negotiations in 1973 with the Copenhagen Declaration on European Identity, which formally defined it as a concept based on the principles of representative democracy, the rule of law, social justice and respect for human rights.[41] This abstract and heavily political conception of European identity has changed very little over the years. It was reaffirmed in the Reflection Group Report for the last Inter-Governmental Conference, which saw the EU as a 'unique design based on common values: the principles of democracy, human rights and social justice'. This way of thinking about European identity is often fused in the literature of integration with elements of European history. Thus, Roman law, political democracy, parliamentary institutions, Judaeo-Christian ethics, the Renaissance, humanism, rationalism, empiricism, romanticism and classicism are mixed together with key personalities from Descartes to Beethoven to construct a European cultural heritage.[42]

At various times, the EU has sought to develop a concrete manifestation of this hoped-for common identity. The most impressive attempt followed the European summit at Fontainebleau in 1984, where a committee chaired by the Italian MEP Pietro Adonino was charged with making recommendations to enhance the public sense of European identity. The Adonino Committee suggested a host of concrete measures: a common television area with more co-production between member states' networks; a Euro-lottery; youth exchanges; an increased European dimension in education policy; the twinning of towns across the Community; the formation of European sports teams; the establishment of a European Academy of Science, Technology and Art; reductions for admission to museums and cultural events; better dissemination of information on EU matters; an EU programme of voluntary work camps for young people; greater cooperation and mobility in higher education; the introduction in all member states of stamps which highlight the EU; and, finally, the adoption of the circle of gold stars with a blue background as the Community's emblem and flag, and the theme of the fourth movement of Beethoven's Ninth Symphony as the Community's anthem. In 1987, the Commission proposed additional measures including the celebration of Europe Day on the ninth of May, organising European weeks, the introduction of a Community driving licence and the development of European 'journeys of awareness'.

The implementation of these measures has been patchy. Although some, such as Erasmus (a scheme for student

'Tell the story of any European city and you give its citizens a European identity. Take the city of Breslau. It used to be 100% German. It was evacuated by the Nazis, then bombed and repopulated after the war with Silesians. Look at the text books, you find a German history or a Polish history. But look at the facts and you find a multi-national history: Polish, Jewish, Bohemian, Austrian, Prussian, German.' *Professor Norman Davies,* Wolfson College, Oxford

exchanges between European universities which facilitates the mutual recognition of course credits and provides grants for students), Comett and Lingua, (which offer grants to take language courses in other European countries), have been successful, the overall record has been unimpressive. Too often attempts at cooperation have tried to create an 'Esperanto' identity of the lowest common denominator. Thus European co-productions have mixed actors and directors from different member states and hollowed out all local references to create films so bland and alien that they appealed to nobody. The creation of European symbols has succeeded in making the European project more visible. Indeed, as many as 80 per cent of EU citizens recognise the flag, but it has failed to build an identity.[43] What was missing was an over-arching narrative that linked the symbols to European integration and gave the identity a content.

The narrative of cultural highlights and political identity has failed to grip the popular imagination. While most people respect the political values it enshrines, they are values which have become universal and do not say something distinctive about Europe. They are also values which most people are more likely to associate with the nation state (a more visible and familiar guardian) than the EU. Above all, these values are so abstract and general that they say very little about our everyday lives. The cultural narrative is not only abstract but elitist as well. It offers a heritage that is recognisable only to a tiny class of intellectuals and is largely meaningless to the majority of Europeans.

In any case, there are real problems with trying to construct a European identity on the nation state model. Above all, the main impetus for the development of national identity was war — the need to collect taxes to raise armies. If the past 50 years of European history have taught us anything, it is the danger of searching for an identity against the 'other', either within or outside European territory. Another problem with the EU's identity projects is that they have failed to recognise that many of the cultural associations that people from Charlemagne to Jean Monnet have chosen in the past to invoke a European identity are no longer available. Christianity cannot occupy an exclusive place at the heart of a European identity both because large numbers of Europeans are not Christian, and because more than half of all Europeans think that formal religion no longer plays an important role in society.[44] Democracy, as argued above, is a value and a practice that is shared around the world, and – in the late 1990s – is more likely to be associated with Washington DC than Athens. Basing identity on ethnicity is also a dangerous strategy; and Europe is becoming ever more ethnically diverse, with its traditional Caucasian self-image and being challenged in all member states. Finally, despite the single market, Europe cannot develop a rigid economic identity because its core economic activities are becoming more and more globalised. Many member states now depend heavily on internationalised production networks.

Even more worryingly, European leaders have often seen European identity in conflict with national identity, which runs counter to most Europeans' aspirations. If there is to be a true Euro-identity, it will be a supplement to national identity and other regional, local and associational allegiances, not a replacement for them. If people are to accept a European identity, it must treat Europe's cultural pluralism as an asset, not as a hindrance.

Trying to make Europe popular through more information

The other approach is to enhance Europe's popular appeal by providing more information to citizens about the EU's structures, aims and activities. An underlying assumption here is that the substance of the EU project is sound and that it is merely the presentation which is faulty.

'If you want to make people feel European, you need to make them behave like Europeans more often: by voting for the European Parliament, paying European taxes, watching European sports teams and doing European voluntary service. By taking part in European rituals, people will start to feel European'.
Thomas Jansen, European Commission

EU what? People don't know about the EU

It is true that most people have a very low level of knowledge about the EU. Eight out of ten Europeans admit in survey responses to being 'not very well informed' or 'not informed at all' about the EU, while only one in 50 claims to be 'very well informed'.[45] And the things that people think they know tend to be wildly at variance with the facts. For example, two thirds of UK citizens think that over 5 per cent of UK taxes go to the EU (almost ten times the real net contribution of the 0.6 per cent).[46] Many others believe the numerous 'Euro-myths' that have been propagated in the tabloid press. For example, 34 per cent of UK citizens believe that the EU is banning curved cucumbers, and one in five think the EU is forcing fishermen to wear hairnets.[47]

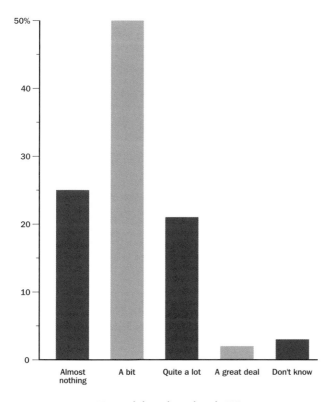

How much do you know about the EU?

Selling the wrong product

It is also true that the EU has not been good at claiming credit for its successes. In fact, a 1993 report by a 'group of experts on information and communication policy' for the Commission made the point that the EU has often been its own worst enemy in making people aware of its achievements. They accuse the Commission and some of the member states of 'selling the wrong product', highlighting technical procedures such as the Treaty of Rome, the Single European Act and the Treaty of Maastricht, rather than the benefits that flow from them: 'Treaty texts are far too technical and remote from daily life for people to understand or even want to understand them. It is a mistake to try to "sell Maastricht" instead of the beneficial effects for me that will result from the European Union.'[48]

There is a danger of these mistakes being repeated in the future. The EU plans to spend millions of ECU on 'information campaigns' educating the business community and citizens about the consequences of a European single currency. While such preparations will be vital to ensuring a successful transition to a single currency, it is important that these campaigns are not the only face that the EU presents to the European public. Polling evidence suggests that the campaigns conducted around the 1992 programme in the run-up to the single market failed to enhance the EU's reputation. Instead they actually damaged it by drawing attention to the reams of regulations that were being forced through the Council of Ministers, reinforcing the Commission's undeserved reputation as an outsize bureaucracy.[49] The EU should therefore be wary of high profile campaigns for a single currency which are unsupported by communications which pay attention to public concerns and priorities. Rather than increasing support for EMU, they are more likely to attract attention to those elements of integration which people support the least.

The key problem, as the group of experts reported, is that there is no central body in charge of communicating with the outside world. Instead of a single, clear message, the press are inundated with 'jargon-filled messages that are not relevant to peoples' lives'. One senior official explained: 'each DG [Directorate General] has an information consultant with their own agenda to promote. The result is total chaos. DG14 sends a fish lorry around Europe to persuade people to "eat more sardines". Another DG sends a train to Waterloo to promote Parma ham and Wensleydale. DG15 gets bored of the single market and decides to do rights. So they organise the "Citizens First" campaign, but don't involve any of the DGs who are in charge with the citizenship agenda – DG5 (in charge of rights), DG7 (transport) or DG24 (consumer affairs).'

This lack of coordination in Brussels also sends out confusing messages to the network of offices in member states. As a Commission official commented: 'Different offices have radically different agendas. We spend a lot of time rebutting Eurosceptic scare stories, but the Italian climate is so different that the Rome office unbelievably sees its role more as promoting scepticism.'

Missing the point

Finally, it is true that the EU has done many things which are positive and failed to get credit for them. It is clearly important for it to professionalise its communications strategies. But people who put their faith in an information strategy alone are missing the real root of the problems – the fact that the EU is not addressing people's core concerns and priorities. As any marketing expert knows, it does not matter how good your information or advertising campaign is: if the product is wrong, it will not sell. The key issue for the EU is that it needs to reconsider what it is for and listen to the messages – confused and ill-informed though they may be – from the citizens of the Union, rather than bombarding them with more information. The problem with information campaigns has been that the flow of information has all been going in one direction – from the insti-

'Europe is the home of monsters. We've invented the nightmares of the world: Frankenstein, Vampires, Goya's great black monsters, Hitler and Stalin. But we've also invented the world's utopias.'
Phillip Dodd, Institute for Contemporary Arts

tutions to the people. In future, information policy must also focus on developing more dialogue and mechanisms for feedback. In fact, if EU leaders stopped and listened to what people wanted – and actually delivered it – they might find that their information campaigns were more successful.

'If you want Europe to be popular, don't overplay your hand. All the elites said that Europe would create jobs. But when unemployment rose, Europe got it in the neck. That is what happens with unfulfillable promises.'
Paul Jaeger, Sources d'Europe

Reconnecting the EU:
aims and aspirations for a
revitalised European project

To thrive in the next century, the EU needs to close the gulf between itself and its citizens. It needs to embody the qualities people already associate with the continent of Europe, reflect the aspirations of its citizens, deliver tangible benefits to the majority of its citizens, and develop a response to the strategic challenges it is facing. To do this it needs a much clearer sense of direction and identity. It needs new missions that are as compelling as those that have carried it, with astonishing success, through its first half century.

What it has already achieved at one time seemed impossible. In the 1940s and 1950s, few realists believed that 55 years after the second world war western Europe would still be at peace, prosperous and democratic. Few predicted that Europe would end the century arguing about currencies rather than fighting over borders. Now once again Europe needs to marry idealism and practical common sense. It needs to stretch its citizens' sense of what is possible while also delivering successful outcomes in relation to the practical issues that matter to people – job prospects and safer environments above all.

These new missions cannot be constructed out of thin air. They need to build on the things that Europeans value. They need to make sense of the past and point clearly towards the future. They have to offer Europeans things they really want, rather than the political classes' visions of 'ever closer union' into a super-state or superpower.

This is far from impossible. The project of integration in Europe is not inherently unpopular. In fact, there is strong latent support for further integration. Part of the reason is that 'Europe' is no longer experienced just by the elites. Not long ago, few Europeans had much sense of the continent they lived in. Holidays in other countries were expensive, other European cuisines were available only in exclusive restaurants or delicatessen stores and second languages were spoken only by a small minority. Today, anyone can share in Europe, whether through food in the supermarkets, drinks in pubs and bars, cheap holidays or travel. This everyday internationalism means that most people no longer see other Europeans as aliens or enemies. Instead the experience of more open borders, more communication, better education and the lasting peace has made them more at ease with their neighbours. Traditional national identities no longer have the pull they once had. But equally, there is little enthusiasm for a monolithic European identity.

In what follows I set out seven 'narratives' which are about rediscovering both what Europe is, and what it can be in the future. Each narrative begins with what people's sense of Europe is, reflects the ambitions of European citizens suggests how benefits can be spread to the many as well as the few, and deals with the strategic challenges that Europe is facing. The narratives are 'mission statements' for EU leaders. They are interconnected and can provide the basis for new programmes of EU activity to reconnect the project of integration with citizens and communities across Europe. They can also form the basis for communications strategies that will give people a sense of what the EU is for, and what it can achieve in the future.

1. Solutions united

Europe's first task is to rediscover the fundamental source of European integration: the fact that risks that cross borders need solutions that cross borders. This generates a 'story' for the future about nations and peoples coming together to reduce and prevent threats to the good life, forging common institutions instead of conflict.

In the recent past, the EU's greatest success has been its achievement of common security. Europe has had a bitter and often catastrophic history. It has experienced two world wars and a cold war this century. It is now experiencing a succession of small civil wars on its borders.

Peace, and the commitment to peace, has become part of Europe's lifeblood. Although there are differences between those countries with long martial traditions and the smaller nations for which military prowess has been less important, support for peacekeeping strategies is widespread. Eight out of ten Europeans think that peacekeeping missions should be a priority of the EU.[50]

While war has receded to the margins of the EU, preventing war and helping to end wars when they arise has to be a central role for the EU in the future, probably with common armed forces. The failure to respond effectively to Bosnia did enormous damage to Europe's self-confidence. It should not happen again.

But war is not the only risk that demands a common response. Today crime is no longer solely national in scope. An offence taking place on a street corner in Britain may have its roots thousands of miles away; criminal gangs operate across national boundaries so that the proceeds of a crime in one country will be invested in another country; and the drugs trade relies on international networks of criminals. Europe needs to respond in kind, acting transnationally to fight against organised crime.

But it is in relation to the degradation of the environment that the new European agenda is clearest. Europe's ecosys-

'At the heart of all European narratives is the fact that Europe is a continent of small countries facing big problems. It is only by clubbing together that we can overcome them.' *Professor Iréne Heidelberger,* Université Libre de Bruxelles

'Historically the
great icon of
Europe was the
warrior, from
Odysseus
onwards –
today it is the
European
tourist.'
Phillip Dodd,
Institute for
Contemporary
Arts

tems are common resources. When Chernobyl exploded the fall-out was felt all the way from Scandinavia to Scotland. Factory emissions cross frontiers to wreak damage on forests and rivers. The seas of Europe all suffer from what many different nations dump into them.

Yet for all the talk, Europe remains reluctant to accept the implications of how the physical world is organised. Environmental policy remains weak and piecemeal in execution. And while it is right that many environmental issues are dealt with at a national or local level, issues concerning the air, the seas, genetically modified organisms or toxic wastes can no longer be dealt with as if they respected national boundaries.

Europeans already understand the need for new responses to common risks. Seventyone per cent see the fight against drugs as a policy area for European decision-making, 68 per cent favour a European approach to foreign policy, 64 per cent favour European action on the environment and 50 per cent on defence.[51]

This does not mean that Europeans want every issue in this general area to be decided by 'diktats' from Brussels. Indeed, 60 per cent of EU citizens would like the 'EU to be responsible only for matters which national governments cannot deal with'.[52] But Europe's citizens do want 'problems without frontiers' to be dealt with at a European level, and the EU has a clear license to operate in this domain. Measures in support of stronger environmental standards, peacekeeping and prevention and control of international crime could include the development of a pan-European equivalent of the FBI designed to tackle the growth of organised transnational crime on the ground; the establishment of a permanent EU peacekeeping corps drawn from all of the national armed services; or the development of the European Environment Agency into a centre for training in the implementation and evaluation of environmental policies and the enforcement of EU directives across the Union and among applicant states.

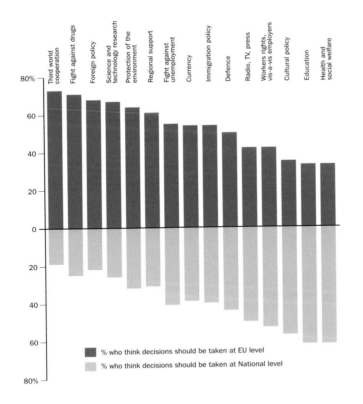

People's natural sense of subsidarity

2. Community of knowledge

In the next century Europe needs to rediscover its role as a creator and disseminator of knowledge, as it enters an era where the economy will primarily be founded on information and knowledge.

Between 1500 and 1950, it led the world as a generator of knowledge, learning and creativity. The great movements of ideas in the renaissance and the enlightenment brought together not only different disciplines — arts, science, philosophy — but also people from different countries. It has also been a leader in democratising access through the printing press and mass education.

Today, knowledge creation, high culture, innovation,

'Europe's most effective export is the ideas that were generated here. The common theme in Western thought is the desire to shape and contract the world, . rather than go with the flow.'
Adam Lury, Howell Henry Chaldcott and Lury

' The adjective 'European' means the spiritual identity that was born with ancient Greek philosophy . . . the passion to know'
Milan Kundera, 'The Art of the Novel'

creativity, fashion, design, and craftsmanship still play an important part in European economies. 79 per cent of European business leaders believe that the European business environment has 'a high level of human capital', 63 per cent that it is 'innovative and enterprising', and 55 per cent that it 'is known for its creative approach in industry'.[53] But although Europe continues to be ahead in many traditional knowledge-based industries (for example, the number of books published per 100,000 in Europe is 108 – over five times as many as in the US), there are fears that at a time when knowledge and human capital are more crucial to Europe's economic future than ever before, Europe is falling behind.

It is falling behind in research and development, spending only $343 per capita a year compared to $604 in Japan and $681 in the USA.[54] It is also falling behind on education and training. Fewer than half of Europeans (46 per cent) think that school prepares children well 'for the rapid changes taking place in our society'.[55] Enrolment and spending on higher education are also behind: only 30 per cent of Europeans enroll in full-time tertiary education compared 66 per cent in the US and 39 per cent in Japan, and spending levels are less than a third of the US and half as much Japan as a percentage of GDP.[56] Europe also feels unprepared for the age of new digital technologies. Only half of Europeans (52 per cent) think that 'schools prepare children well to use the new technologies and the tools of the information society', and four and a half times as many people are connected to the internet in the US as in Europe.[57]

These are all areas of concern to the mass of European citizens. A large majority (72 per cent) think that 'pooling European research efforts' is a priority.[58] In fact, majorities in all fifteen countries think that decisions over science and technology research should be taken at a European rather than a national level (67 per cent Europe-wide agree, 26 per cent disagree).[59] And specific projects such as fighting cancer and AIDS are considered a priority for the EU by 86 per cent of Europeans.[60] Education and training are also central to

Europeans' interests: seven out of ten claim that they would like to continue learning or training throughout their lives – both to improve their qualifications and their general knowledge. And though two thirds see education policy as a national rather than a European area, they see a role for the EU in encouraging a culture of learning and organising cross-border exchanges and co-operation.[61]

So what does this mean for the EU? At the moment not enough of the EU's resources and efforts go into knowledge and its dissemination. Of its 88 billion ECU annual budget, only 4 per cent currently goes to R&D and less than 0.4 per cent to education.[62] Nor is enough done to encourage educational and research links across borders. The Framework programmes have had some success in encouraging more collaboration, particularly in recent years around practical applications, but far too much money was captured by a handful of large companies. The Socrates programme of school and university exchanges has been popular, as is the Erasmus programme that sends 85,000 student across Europe every year. But much more could be done to encourage transnational work placements, educational exchanges and community exchanges, and to expand opportunities to 'experience Europe' beyond the ranks of the most highly qualified. Perhaps more than anything, a common commitment to one or two major projects in relation to learning, such as a Europe-wide Open University or a common research project around major diseases such as cancer or AIDS, would signify that Europe was rediscovering that knowledge has been the foundation of its progress in the past and will be in the future.

3. The travelling continent

For much of its recent history, European policy has concentrated on bringing money and jobs to where people happen to live. By doing so it has reinforced labour immobility. In the future, if the single market and the single currency are

'In all European countries we can observe today a deep crisis in education . . . Even mass education seems unable to transmit basic cultural skills to the children of the less privileged. Inequality, uncertainty and inadaptability are the experience of thousands of families at a much higher, but therefore even more frustrating, level than in the past'.
Professor Robert Picht

'Colonialism lies at the heart of Europeanism. The visibility and membership of diaspora communities dates back to the 18th century. The Blacks in the Dutch world. The tropical museum in Copenhagen or Rotterdam.'
Professor Paul Gillroy, Goldsmith's College London

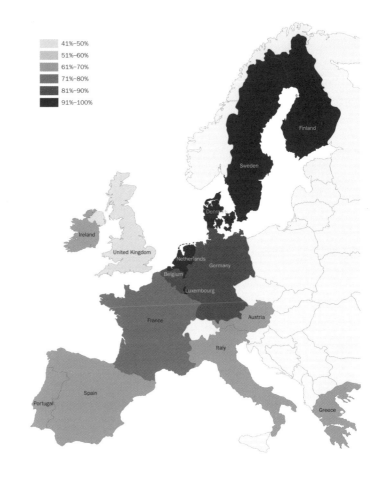

	41%–50%
	51%–60%
	61%–70%
	71%–80%
	81%–90%
	91%–100%

Percentage of young Europeans who speak a second language well enough to have a conversation

really going to work, Europe will need to rediscover its identity as a 'travelling continent'.

In the past Europe was rarely static. Migration for the poor and tourism for the rich have coloured much of its recent history. The legacy of mobility can be seen in the 'Promenade des Anglais' in Nice, the plaques commemorating the lives of such great European migrants as Marx, Freud and Picasso, or the strong remaining links between the French and the Quebecois, the British and the

Australians, the Italians and the Italian-Americans. Europe's explorers mapped the world to an extent unmatched by their Arabic and Chinese predecessors. Marco Polo and Magellan, Cook and Livingstone, were in their own times proof against the idea of an insular, inward looking Europe.

Today Europe remains a surprisingly restless continent. The Grand Tours of the eighteenth century have been replaced by the Interrail and the package tour, and royal marriages by holiday romances (5 per cent of young Europeans went to another EU country in 1996/97 to visit a boyfriend or girlfriend).[63] Although half of Europeans still holiday in their own country, 39 per cent went to another EU country – 20 per cent more than in 1985.[64] The figures for fifteen to 24 year olds are even more impressive: 57 per cent of them had been to another EU country in 1996/97.[65]

This idea of mobility has a powerful resonance for European citizens – especially the younger ones. Asked what the EU meant to them, the single most popular answer among fifteen to 24 year olds was 'the ability to go wherever I want in Europe' – more popular than both 'a means of improving the economic situation in Europe' and 'guaranteed lasting peace in Europe'.[66]

However, in some respects Europe has failed to become more mobile. Only 1.6 per cent of EU citizens are permanent residents in another EU country, and only a third say they would consider taking a good job in another EU country.[67] While this willingness to move rises to 78 per cent among business leaders, most Europeans still do not see the EU as a single market or a single labour market.[68]

The problem is that it is still very difficult for people to be mobile. So far, only the most irritating barriers have been removed. Border controls have been reduced to a minimum, moving of one's personal possessions has been made easier, rights of settlement and right for professionals to practice in other countries were introduced and later extended by rulings by the European Court of Justice (most notably the Bosman ruling that ensured free movement for football

'To understand our history as Europeans is to think back to the "Vanished Kingdoms". Aragon included Sicily, Sardinia, Athens, Naples, and Barcelona. Poland-Lithuania stretched from the Black Sea to the Baltic. 15th century Burgundy was the heart of the original EC. These have almost totally disappeared from the history books. By filling in the blanks not filled by the great powers we can really understand our history as Europeans.' *Professor Norman Davies,* Wolfson College, Oxford

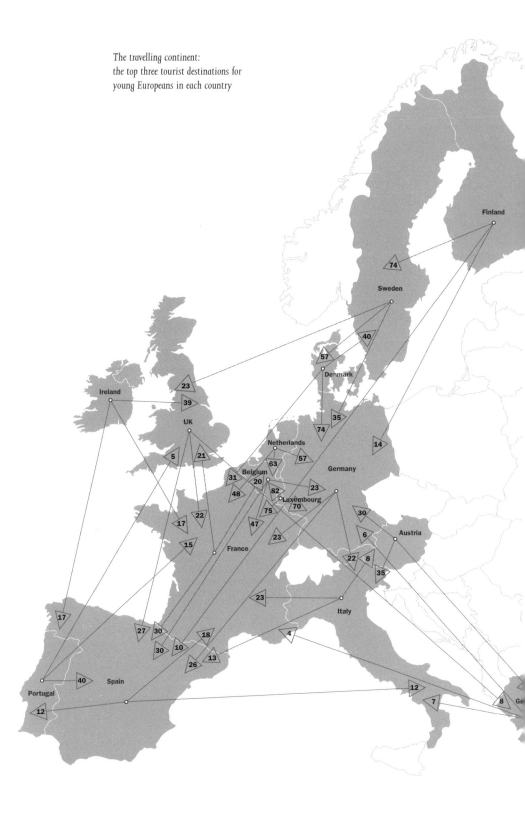

The travelling continent:
the top three tourist destinations for
young Europeans in each country

players). All these were important measures, but they did not provide Europeans with the tools to be mobile, only a negative freedom by removing artificial barriers. They left intact two serious obstacles to mobility.

The most serious one is language. Half of all Europeans, and as many as three out of ten young Europeans, don't speak a second language well enough to have a conversation, while the only language which a considerable proportion do speak is English. As a result, almost 40 per cent of young people in Europe cite a lack of confidence with the language as the main anticipated problem in working or studying abroad.[69] The importance of dealing with this is underlined by the fact that 70 per cent of business leaders think that it is important or very important for their staff to be skilled in other EU languages.[70]

The other obstacle is the continued lack of an integrated and cheap transport system for Europe – even though it was promised in the Treaty of Rome. Moreover, air travel costs remain high relative to the rest of the world, despite some efforts by the European Commission.

To achieve the goal of a truly mobile continent the EU needs to remove the last few technical barriers to mobility, such as the remaining barriers to recognition of professional qualifications. It needs to improve language skills and to integrate access to these more clearly into its labour market policies. And it needs to deregulate air travel and to push forward on trans-European public transport networks.

There may be even be scope for measures such as a European Tourist board to celebrate the culture of mobility. Together these steps will help to make Europeans more at ease with mobility. But perhaps the fundamental change will be to devote as much energy to helping people move to new jobs, or new relationships, as in the past has been devoted to keeping people where they were.

'The strongest European unifier has been the rise of the au pair girl moving around Europe in temporary jobs, picking up languages and culture wherever they go'.
Professor Eric Hobsbawm, Birbeck College, London

4. Urban Hymns

'If Europe is a network, its nodes are cities. The source of its ideas, its culture, its revolutions. The future of the continent has to be as a Europe of the cities'.
Richard Rogers,
Richard Rogers Partnership

'As we approach the end of the century our cities are becoming the focus of a host of pressing social, economic and environmental problems. Social exclusion threatens the very basis of our society.'
Monika Wulf Mathies,
European Commission

Although eight out of ten Europeans live in cities, most of the EU's budget is spent on the countryside, primarily through farm subsidies. In the future Europe will need to rediscover its urbanity.

Cities have been the lifeblood of the European continent. They have been the places where people 'lived their ideas, needs, aspirations, dreams, projects, conflicts, memories, anxieties, loves, passions, obsessions and fears'.[71] They have been the cosmopolitan heartlands of new ideas, progress and revolution, new industries and new technologies.

At times Europe's political structures have been organised around its cities: from ancient Greece to medieval Italy, and from the Hanseatic league to the numerous twinning arrangements and networks of cities that are in operation today.

But many European cities are now in crisis. Most have seen a sharp increase in levels of crime and fear of crime. Many people are frequently afraid to go out at night or allow their children to walk to school. They have suffered from persistent environmental problems, in particular poor air quality and traffic congestion. And in recent years they have borne the brunt of deindustrialisation, so that most of the areas of acute social exclusion are in and around the EU's major cities.

Yet in practice the EU sometimes seems to have forgotten that it presides over a largely urbanised continent. It continues to be run more in the interests of the 6.5 per cent of farmers, than the 80 per cent of city dwellers. The most obvious manifestation of this is the fact that 48 per cent of the EU budget is spent on the Common Agricultural Policy. But there are also subtler ways that the EU has failed to take its urban nature seriously. The region, rather than the city, has been promoted through the application of the subsidiarity principle in EU economic and social programmes under the structural funds. The institutionalisation of regions in the

European cities by night

decision-making process has produced a consistent bias against city-driven solutions, and a failure to give adequate backing to the political and administrative leaders of Europe's cities.

Yet, in the future, there are strong signs that cities will become even more important as economic powerhouses. As nation states become less important, cities look set to recapture their confidence; to develop more independent industrial and economic policies; to pursue their competitive advantages; and to deal with the problems of environmental quality and social division that national and regional governments have often failed to tackle.

The European Union should welcome and encourage an urban renaissance. It should clearly signal steps to shift resources from the countryside to cities, while targeting rural support much more intelligently, as well as to rethink the balance between regional and urban support in the structural funds. And it should give a higher profile and status to the many existing, and often very imaginative, programmes to celebrate Europe's cities and share their best ideas. It could also look at providing a voice for city leaders, maybe through a 'Forum of Mayors' to complement the Committee of the Regions.

5. Solidarity

Europe has led the world in showing how societies can reach accommodations between different classes. While other societies rested on dictatorship or hierarchy, or suffered wide inequalities, Europe has succeeded in achieving both economic growth and social solidarity. It now needs to redefine what that means in a new environment, that of globalisation of economic competition, in which solidarity and policies for mitigating the effect of market forces on labour, communities and the environment have to spread beyond the confines of the nation.

The values that lead to the formation of welfare states are

still central to the way Europe sees itself. 65 per cent of Europeans agree that the 'Government should be making sure that the tax system redistributes income from the better-off to the less well-off', while only 16 per cent disagree.[72] And 80 per cent of business leaders think that one of the distinctive things about the European business environment is that it is 'concerned about the social welfare of its workers'.[73] On the surface at least, these powerful feeling of solidarity are not restricted to the national level. As far as the public are concerned the two top priorities for the EU are fighting unemployment and tackling poverty and social exclusion.[74]

However these latent feelings of cross-border solidarity have not been nurtured. Many people in countries that are net contributors to the EU are becoming increasingly restless about the extent of their contributions. Forty per cent of Europeans fear that rich member states will have to pay more for poor ones, and this figure rises to 55 per cent in net contributor countries such as Germany and the Netherlands.[75] There is also only lukewarm support for enlargement – partly because of higher costs and fears of losing regional aid. There are small majorities in favour of widening the EU to include Poland (43 per cent for, 34 per cent against), Hungary (41 per cent for, 33 per cent against), the Czech Republic (41 per cent for, 33 per cent against) and Cyprus (40 per cent for, 33 per cent against), and small majorities against granting membership to the other applicant countries.[76]

These limits to cross-border solidarity are in part a symptom of the EU's broader problems. People resent making contributions because they believe that the money will simply be 'wasted' on farmers and fishermen. Resentment also feeds off exaggerated views of how much is spent: two thirds of UK citizens think that over 5 per cent of UK taxes go to the EU – almost ten times the real net contribution of 0.6 per cent.[77]

So how can the EU build on this latent solidarity? The

'Europe has created the most comprehensive network of state support in education, health care and social security that exists. Provision varies from country to country, but even people in the poorer parts of western Europe have a vastly better system of welfare care than exists anywhere else in the world, with the possible exception of Japan'. *Hamish Macrae*, 'The World of 2020'

most important step will be to relate spending priorities more clearly to public concerns in relation to jobs, the common risks outlined earlier and quality of life, and then to ensure that money spent is tied to clear goals and targets. Redistribution will always be more legitimate if it is efficient and dynamic, rather than creating relations of dependency between poorer and richer areas. Getting this right is a matter of politics and language as well as of specific policy measures. In the longer run, European leaders will need to start talking about their fellow Europeans not as supplicants but as citizens deserving investment and opportunities to bring the prospects of poorer communities more closely into line with those of the rich ones.

6. The good life

When people think of European institutions they think of bureaucracy, red-tape and grey officials. But when they think of Europe they think of the good life – sun, sea, olive oil, wine, chocolates, beer, and holidays.

While some parts of east Asia and America might be more prosperous in purely financial terms, there is arguably a much better balance between work and leisure, better public services and a richer culture in Europe. Large minorities may not be sharing in much of that good life, but for centuries, even millennia, Europeans have been actively pursuing better ways of living. Today, Europe remains the only area of the world where even the unemployed can maintain a decent standard of living.

Europe's economy reflects this connection to the good life. European industries are famous for it: fashion, design, food and wine from Italy; perfume, haute couture, food and wine from France; chocolates and beer from Belgium; luxury cars from Germany; whisky, films, fashion and fiction from the UK; high quality modern consumer products from Scandinavia; holidays in Spain and Portugal.

But people are coming to have a broader idea of what

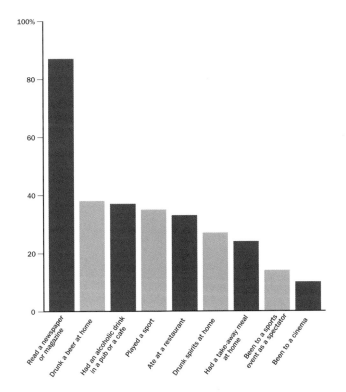

100%

80

60

40

20

0

Read a newspaper or magazine

Drunk a beer at home

Had an alcoholic drink in a pub or a cafe

Played a sport

Ate at a restaurant

Drunk spirits at home

Had a take-away meal at home

Been to a sports event as a spectator

Been to a cinema

Activities Europeans will undertake in a week

'Europe is rich in quality of life. It has managed to create a lifestyle, or rather, a variety of lifestyles, which the rest of the world finds deeply enviable. Out of the five largest tourist destinations, three are in western Europe: France, Spain and Italy. Between them, they attract more foreign visitors than the whole of North America'. *Hamish Macrae,* 'The World in 2020'

makes life good. Getting the balance right between work and leisure is extremely important for Europeans. They work less hours a week than their counterparts in the US and Japan: 33 compared to 35 and 43 respectively.[78] And one in four worry regularly about not having enough free time (rising to 31 per cent among 16–24 year olds).[79] They also see their local environment as part of their quality of life and are willing to make a concerted effort to improve it. Two thirds of Europeans claim that they recycle many of the products they buy, and 62 per cent claim to buy products made of recycled material whenever possible.[80] These claims are borne out by the facts – Europeans recycle 46 per cent of the paper and cardboard they consume and 49 per cent of glass, compared with 34 and 22 per cent in the US.[81]

But the same people do not associate the institutions of the EU with their quality of life. When asked what the EU will have brought about in ten years time, only one in four (23 per cent) of young Europeans said 'a better quality of life for most people'.[82] Europe's leaders have failed to project a compelling vision of what the good life might mean for Europe's citizens – that mix of prosperity, a sustainable environment and a balance between the demands of economic life and social bonds that is so attractive to citizens from Finland to Portugal.

In the future, the EU will need to direct its attentions more closely to what it can do to improve people's quality of life. That may mean more measures on working hours and time off. It may mean more efforts to support nations and regions in developing areas of natural beauty (maybe through protected European Parks), and it may mean extending research and development programmes to recognise that ways of living are as much sources of economic advantage as technology and patents. But it will mean above all projecting an attainable vision of how life could be better.

7. The European mosaic

Europe is a patchwork of different cultures, religions, languages and views. But too many of its leaders have wanted to give Europe the homogeneity of a classic nation state, with a common (usually high) culture, common currency, common firms and a common constitution. Yet Europe's future lies in being something very different from a nation state writ large. Its strength lies in creating a common space in which diversity can flourish.

The first site of diversity is Europe's people or, more accurately, peoples. By and large, Europeans are tolerant of diversity: eight out of ten (81 per cent) claim not to be disturbed at all by people of another race, while 83 per cent claim not to be disturbed by people of different nationalities.[83] For young people, this tolerance is even more pronounced –

'The US created a big market by standardising and universalising beliefs, allegiances and value systems. It paid a high price in conformity. The EU's big chance is to create a dialogue out of the Kaleidoscope of cultures and polyglot identities that make it up'.
Charles Hampden Turner, Judge Institute of Management, Cambridge

only 3 per cent feel uneasy with people from another nationality, culture or religion, while just 5 per cent say that they feel uneasy with people of different races.[84] One in five young people even felt that their nationality's population 'has always consisted of people of foreign descent', while one in four thought that foreigners should have the same rights as nationals.[85]

Europeans recognise and value this diversity. Fifty four per cent of Europeans agree with the statement 'Europe will never be one country because of the differences between us and other Europeans', while only 20 per cent disagree.[86] This is a warning against the rhetoric often deployed by European governments and officials. Every time a European leader makes a speech about constructing a 'European nation', or a 'federalist Europe', or the commission issues a car sticker proclaiming 'mon pays – l'Europe', unwarranted fears of homogeneity are fuelled.

The second site of diversity is the economy. In consumer electronics, Phillips provides the main competition to Japan and East Asia. In civil aviation, Airbus is Boeing's main competitor in airframes and Rolls Royce challenges General Electric for engines. The three largest chemical companies in the world are German and the fourth is British. Seven out of the top ten pharmaceutical companies are European. Europe also has the largest motor industry in the world. And France and the UK are the biggest exporters of conventional arms after Russia and the USA.

The development of the EU economy has not come about as a result of a central plan. The process of specialisation has happened naturally as a result of competition between countries, historical accidents and the effects of everything from climate to geography. Although the Commission and national governments have often tried to encourage mergers and joint ventures to exploit economies of scale, its efforts to go against the pluralist grain have rarely been successful and Europe's most successful industries have developed organically.

'The only historical moment of European identity was the Roman Empire other attempts have simply been to rebuild it. This empire was multi-ethnic and multi-national and no-one tampered with local identities'.
César Vidal

'European identity is not univocal, it is a complex of multiple identities'.
Alberto Elordi, Fundacíon Alternativas

The third site of diversity is culture. Over a third of Europeans fear losing their national identity and culture as a result of European integration. When the EU has not respected national idiosyncrasies in devising regulations, it has fuelled hostility to the EU. In the UK, for example, perceived threats to double decker buses, the 'British loaf' and British chocolate have done damage to the EU's reputation. The result is that 54 per cent of people in the UK say they are afraid of losing their national identity and culture as a result of European integration.

The EU now needs to shed its image as a homogenising force. It needs to end the 'one size fits all' approach to policy-making, not least because as the EU grows, it will become increasingly difficult to devise policies which suit all countries at all times. It needs to be more careful about respecting national idiosyncrasies when devising regulations. And it needs to project an image of Europe that not only encompasses Dutch farmers and Swedish office workers, Orthodox Greeks and Protestant Scots, but also the new Europeans: the Turks of Germany, Algerians of France, Pakistanis of Britain, as well as the future immigrants who will become a hugely important force in providing new energy for a 'greying' continent whose population is now stable and even falling.

'Businesses in Europe are increasingly multi-cultural and multi-national. Their identities need to reflect this to work in a European context as well as locally, nationally and globally.'
Frances Newell, Interbrand Newell and Sorrell

Seven missions for the future of Europe

Each of these stories is based on the lifestyle, values and priorities of Europeans. They build on Europe's past, but they provide a clear agenda for the future. Together they can be the basis for a new sense of direction to European integration, and they can help EU leaders show what might lie at the heart of a rediscovered European identity.

Conclusion

We are only a few years away from the fiftieth anniversary of the Treaty of Rome. By almost any criteria this ranks as one of the most successful treaties ever signed. It has delivered steadily rising prosperity and a civic underpinning for peace in a continent used to war. And it has done so without the conspiracies against democracy of earlier orders, like the post-Napoleonic settlement.

Yet it is now far harder to imagine where the EU is going, or what might be done to celebrate that anniversary, than it has been for some time. Even the historic enlargement to the East and the establishment of EMU Union have become embroiled in technical wranglings, and there is no longer a clear sense of what the EU is integrating for. Certainly, we associate it with free markets, democratic elections, the rule of law and a common heritage of high culture, but where does this leave everything from its military policies to its approach to Hollywood movies or Internet pornography, its stance on drugs or unemployment?

The technocratic vision of Europe as a set of neutral rules governing competition, harmonisation, money and budgets is no longer enough to generate legitimacy. It is too thin, austere and distant from people's lives and priorities. It cannot inspire European citizens like the earlier promises of peace and prosperity. In its next phase Europe needs to break from this pattern of integration 'from above'. It needs to become a people's Europe based on the priorities and values of its citizens rather than seeing them as an afterthought, and it needs to harness their aspirations in meeting the massive challenges – economic, ecological and social – of the new century.

In practical terms, that means reorienting its agenda much more clearly to the borderless problems, hopes and solutions that matter to its citizens. In presentational terms, it means tapping into the strong strata of potential support that 'Europe' does command. The two need to be seen as different sides of the same coin. In the modern world presentation and content have to be integrated.

The narratives set out in this report show that there is an attractive and sophisticated agenda waiting to be defined. They deal with the challenges to Europe's prosperity, its environment and its sense of solidarity. Together they are as bold as the missions that Europe embarked on after 1945. Europe's citizens want to believe that they can work. They want to rediscover a Europe that they can believe in. It's up to policy makers to deliver it.

'There is a myth that British people have stronger links with the US than with Europe. In fact we only share language, films and McDonalds. The list of things we don't share is much longer: values, cars, heritage, tastes, sports, leisure and the environment. These are all things which Europe has in common'.
Chris Haskins, Northern Foods

Notes

[1] Eurovisions: new dimensions of European integration, Demos Collection 13, 1998, Demos, London
[2] Leonard M, 1997, Politics without frontiers: the role of political parties in Europe's future, Demos, London
[3] Hix S, The political system of the European Union, to be published in 1999, Macmillan, London; Gabl M, 1997, Interests and integration: market liberalization, public opinion and European Union, University of Michigan Press, Michigan
[4] Christie I, 1998, 'Sustaining Europe', Eurovisions: New dimensions of European integration, Demos Collection 13, Demos, London; Leonard M, 1998, Making Europe popular: the search for European identity, Demos, London
[5] Cooper R, 1996, The Post-Modern State and the World Order, Demos, London
[6] Directorate General X, 1998, Eurobarometer: public opinion in the European Union, report no 48, European Commission, Brussels
[7] Directorate General X, 1997, Eurobarometer: Public Opinion in the European Union, report no 47, European Commission, Brussels
[8] see note 2
[9] see note 7
[10] see note 7
[11] Foreign and Commonwealth Office 1998, Europe Polling, unpublished, carried out by Gould, Greenberg, Carville International
[12] McKie A, 1998, 'How European are we?', Eurovisions: new dimensions of European integration, Demos Collection 13, Demos, London
[13] see note 7
[14] Directorate General X, 1996, Eurobarometer: public opinion in the European Union, report no 45, European Commission, Brussels
[15] European Commission, 1997, Eurostat yearbook, European Commission, Luxembourg
[16] see note 15
[17] New tastes and eating habits in Europe: change and opportunity for food manufacturers prepared for BMP DDB Needham, 1997, London
[18] see note 15
[19] Castells M, 1997, The End of Millennium, Blackwell, Oxford
[20] see note 6
[21] see note 6
[22] see note 11
[23] see note 3; the decision-makers responses are from the Directorate General X, 1996, Top decision-makers survey, European Commission, Brussels; the ordinary citizens

come from Directorate General X, 1996, Eurobarometer: public opinion in the European Union, report no 46, European Commission, Brussels

[24] see note 23

[25] see note 23

[26] see note 6

[27] see note 6

[28] see note 7

[29] Reif K, 1993, 'Cultural convergence and cultural diversity as factors in European identity' in Garcia S, 1993, European identity and the search for legitimacy, Pinter, London.

[30] Handley D, 1981, 'Public opinion and European integration: the crisis of the 1970s', European journal of political research, volume 9; Wallace H, 1993, 'Deepening and widening: problems of legitimacy for the EC', in Garcia S, 1993, European identity and the search for legitimacy, Pinter, London.

[31] Directorate General XXII, 1997, Young Europeans, European Commission, Brussels.

[32] see note 7

[33] August 1996 European Movement data in Britain and the European Union, research study conducted by MORI, unpublished.

[34] see note 33; see note 29; Leonard D, 1998, The Economist guide to the European Union, 5th edition, The Economist Books, London; Butler D, 1979, 'Public Opinion and Community Membership' in The Political Quarterly, vol 50, 151–156

[35] MORI, October 1997

[36] Opinion Research Business, 1997, Britain and the EU: what people think, ORB, London, carried out for the European Commission

[37] MORI/European Movement, June 1996, Public attitudes to Europe and the European Union, MORI / European Movement, unpublished

[38] Synergy Brand Values Ltd, Insight 97: a survey into social change, BMRB, London

[39] see note 7

[40] see note 12

[41] Copenhagen Summit conference, 1973, pp.118–119

[42] Smith A D, 1992 'National Identity and the Idea of European Unity' in International Affairs

[43] see note 14

[44] Picht R, 1993, 'Disturbed identities: Social and Cultural Mutations in Contemporary Europe' in Garcia S, 1993, European identity and the search for legitimacy, Pinter, London.

[45] see note 6

[46] see note 11

[47] see note 33

[48] de Clercq W, 1993, *Reflection on Information and Communication Policy of the European Union*, European Commission, Brussels

[49] see note 44

[50] see note 14

[51] see note 6

[52] see note 6

[53] Demos / Interbrand Newell and Sorrell, June 1998, *European Business Leaders Survey*, unpublished, London

[54] DTI

[55] see note 14

[56] United Nations, *United Nations Human Development Index (UNHDI)*, 1997, United Nations

[57] see note 6; see note 56

[58] see note 6

[59] see note 6

[60] see note 6

[61] see note 6

[62] see note 15

[63] see note 31

[64] see note 6

[65] see note 31

[66] see note 31

[67] Henley Centre, 1997, *Frontiers*, Henley Centre, London

[68] see note 53

[69] see note 31

[70] see note 53

[71] Bianchini F and Landry C, 1996, *The Creative City*, Demos, London

[72] see note 67

[73] see note 53

[74] see note 6

[75] see note 6

[76] see note 6

[77] see note 11

[78] see note 56

[79] see note 67

[80] see note 67

[81] see note 56

[82] see note 31

[83] see note 6

[84] see note 31

[85] see note 31

[86] see note 67